TOGETHER IN PERFECT FELICITY

A PRIDE AND PREJUDICE VARIATION

P. O. DIXON

Together in Perfect Felicity

A Pride and Prejudice Variation

Copyright © 2019 by P. O. Dixon

All rights reserved.

No part of this book may be reproduced in any form or by any electronic or mechanical means, including information storage and retrieval systems, without written permission from the author, except for the use of brief quotations in a book review.

This book is a work of fiction. The characters depicted in this book are fictitious or are used fictitiously. Any resemblance to actual events, locales, or persons, living or dead, is entirely coincidental.

ISBN-13: 9781795454346

DEDICATION

To Pepper, who came into our lives and filled us all with even more joy!

ACKNOWLEDGMENTS

Heartfelt gratitude is bestowed to Miss Jane Austen for her timeless classic, *Pride and Prejudice*, which makes all this possible. What a joy it is imagining different paths to happily ever after for our beloved couple, Darcy and Elizabeth, and then sharing the stories with the world.

Special thanks to Betty and Michele for all you do.

CONTENTS

Chapter 1	1
Chapter 2	11
Chapter 3	17
Chapter 4	25
Chapter 5	33
Chapter 6	39
Chapter 7	49
Chapter 8	57
Chapter 9	65
Chapter 10	71
Chapter 11	79
Chapter 12	85
Chapter 13	93
Chapter 14	105
Chapter 15	113
Chapter 16	123
Chapter 17	129
Chapter 18	143
Chapter 19	153
Chapter 20	161
Chapter 21	167
Chapter 22	173
Chapter 23	179
Chapter 24	185
Chapter 25	191
Chapter 26	199
Chapter 27	209

Chapter 28	219
Also by P. O. Dixon	225
About the Author	229
Featured Book Excerpt	231

"Do anything rather than marry without affection."

Jane Austen

CHAPTER 1

IN WANT OF DIVERSION

*I*t is a truth universally acknowledged that the topic of discussion among four unmarried young ladies who are gathered together in the same room and in want of diversion must invariably center on the prospects for marital felicity for each of them in their turn. Such was indeed the case in Miss Elizabeth Bennet's bedroom at Longbourn manor that day.

"I contend that happiness in marriage is entirely a matter of chance," declared Charlotte Lucas, who was visiting from the neighboring village.

"Spoken by the least likely of the four of us to reach the altar."

Elizabeth, the second eldest of five Bennet

daughters, stared at her cousin in utter dismay on behalf of her intimate friend, Charlotte. Elizabeth's junior by two years, Phoebe Phillips paid her no notice. Not that Elizabeth expected any real sort of regret on the young lady's part. If ever one might be described as her mother's daughter, unquestionably, it was Phoebe. Though closest in age to Elizabeth's younger sister Mary and closest in terms of sensibility to Elizabeth's two youngest sisters, Kitty and Lydia, Phoebe much preferred the company of the two eldest Bennet sisters, Jane and Elizabeth.

What with Phoebe being the only daughter of Mrs. Agatha Phillips, and Mrs. Phillips being the only sister of Mrs. Fanny Bennet, it was generally expected that the cousins would be the dearest of friends, even if the girls' temperaments were as varying as day and night. To her credit, Phoebe was not quite so vulgar as her mother was thought to be. Elizabeth rather supposed it was merely a matter of time.

Whereas the embarrassment of it all caused the eldest Bennet daughter's angelic face to redden, the younger daughter's astonishment was not so easily repressed.

"Phoebe!" Elizabeth exclaimed with energy.

"What did I say that is not true?"

"It is not what you said so much as it is the manner in which you said it. You owe Charlotte an apology," Elizabeth declared.

A very plain-looking, intelligent woman and the oldest in the group by at least four years, Charlotte said, "Dearest Eliza, you need not censure your cousin on my behalf."

Phoebe smirked. "There, you see, Lizzy," the young lady cried, "Charlotte knows the truth when she hears it. She is not at all offended."

"Heaven forbid," replied Charlotte. "Were I to be affronted by any of the things you say, Phoebe, I might be as miserable as you are."

Pleased by her friend's retort, even at her own relation's expense, Elizabeth covered her mouth to mask her smile. She loved nothing more than laughing at the ridiculousness of others: a trait she inherited from her dear father, Mr. Thomas Bennet.

Jane's disposition demanded a more amicable resolution to the ebbing tension among their little group. "I believe no one is ever really too old to find happiness in marriage," said she.

"Says the second least likely person among us to find a husband."

"Phoebe!" Elizabeth exclaimed once more.

"Although, I will allow that Jane is the only one of us who has ever come close to securing a marriage proposal. How many times have we heard my aunt Bennet boast of the young man at my uncle Gardiner's home in town who was so much in love with her and the general belief that he would have made her an offer even though he did not?"

"Lest you forget, Phoebe, Jane was only fifteen at the time. I recall Mrs. Bennet saying that likely was the reason," Charlotte said.

"Oh, but he wrote such pretty verses on her," Phoebe waxed poetically. "Pray, whatever became of your young beau, Cousin Jane?"

Elizabeth said, "Who really gives a care? Poetry or no poetry, the man is no doubt a fool."

Charlotte scoffed. "I wager all men are fools. How else might one explain the abundance of single young ladies in want of husbands among our general acquaintances?"

"Owe it to our rather exacting standards," Elizabeth promptly asserted. "That and the limited variety of single young men in this part of the country."

"Exacting? Pray what exactly is your opinion on the ideal husband, Lizzy?" Phoebe asked.

"I should like to think the ideal husband is respectable and kind and one who honors his wife and protects his family."

"And handsome—"

Her spirits rising to playfulness, Elizabeth said, "I see no reason why the ideal husband should not be handsome. I posit one might just as easily fall in love with a handsome man as one who is rather less pleasing to the eye. Handsome men deserve love too."

"Oh, Lizzy!" Jane said in response to her sister's jest.

"It is not as though you need ever concern yourself in that regard, Jane. You are far too beautiful to catch the eye of any man whose beauty does not equal yours."

"How a gentleman looks on the outside can mean nothing at all if he does not possess goodness within," Jane said.

"I could not agree more," Charlotte began, "and as we all know how much Eliza enjoys professing opinions that are not always her own, she surely does not measure a man by his physical attributes either."

"Indeed," Elizabeth said, reaching out to take her friend by the hand and giving it a gentle squeeze in solidarity. "You know me very well." Releasing her friend's hand, she continued, "But that is enough about me. What characteristics do you look for in a potential husband, dearest Charlotte?"

Charlotte shrugged. "I always like to think of myself as being a very sensible woman. At seven and twenty, I have long given up the idea of meeting my very own charming prince. So long as I can marry a decent man and be the mistress of my own home, however large or small, I should have no cause to repine."

"La!" exclaimed Phoebe. "Decent. Respectable. Handsome. If neither of you is willing to say what is the most important characteristic of the ideal husband, then I surely will."

"What else is there?" Jane asked.

"Why the gentleman must be rich, of course!"

"Surely you have heard it said that money does not buy happiness, Phoebe," Elizabeth said.

"I have heard it said time and time again, and I simply do not believe it. And on the oft chance it is true, what does it signify, especially since one might just as easily fall in love with a rich man as a poor one."

"Says the youngest of the four of us," Elizabeth responded.

"If by that you mean to say I am merely young and foolish, perhaps I am, but I shall not be deterred from my opinion. Besides, as Charlotte said, happiness in marriage is purely a matter of chance. I prefer to take my chances with a rich man."

"I wish you nothing but the best of luck," Elizabeth said.

"Laugh at me if you dare, Cousin Lizzy, but I seriously doubt there is one among us who would refuse the hand of a wealthy gentleman, regardless of his character."

Elizabeth did not mean to be cruel, but she could not help but laugh a little. She threw a quick glance to her right and then another to her left. "In spite of your strong resolve, your assertion is one that will no doubt go unproven. It is not as though there is an abundance of wealthy young men in want of wives in our midst."

Phoebe clutched a soft pillow to her bosom. "Surely you are aware that particular dilemma is soon to be resolved."

"Are you speaking of the imminent arrival of Mr. Charles Bingley—the young man who recently let Netherfield Park?" Jane inquired.

"Indeed, I am. To be more precise, the young man of large fortune from the north of England. He is said to have five thousand pounds a year, and he is also said to be handsome, which must surely count for something with you, Lizzy. But wait until you hear the best part of it all. Mr. Bingley will be accompanied by a rather large party when he returns. He is single, after all, and where there is one single man there is bound to be another and another and another."

"What can the size of Mr. Bingley's party have to do with any of us?" cried Jane.

"The greater the number of single men in his party, the better are our chances of meeting our potential husbands among them," Phoebe cried. She tilted her head in a moment of contemplation and then continued. "Oh! I have a brilliant idea. What say you, ladies, that we make a pact that the four of us will do everything in our power to find husbands during the course of the next twelve months?"

"Even if what you propose were viable, marriage is a serious commitment. I do not know that I would be comfortable approaching such a consequential endeavor in such a frivolous—dare I say tactless—manner as you are suggesting."

"For heaven's sake, Lizzy, it is not as though I have suggested a wager or anything of the sort. I am merely suggesting that we seize control of our own destinies. If not now, then when? None of us is getting any younger, and who is to say? One of us might very well succeed.

"Think about it, Charlotte... Jane... Lizzy. What is there for any of us to lose?"

CHAPTER 2

IN DUE TIME

LONDON, ENGLAND - DARCY HOUSE, 1811

"Brother, may I be allowed to travel with you to Hertfordshire? I promise you will scarcely be aware of my presence."

Fitzwilliam Darcy laid his newspaper aside, thus giving his younger sister his full attention. "Georgiana, you know how much it pains me to cause you displeasure, but in this case, I fear I have no other choice."

"What would be the harm in my joining you and the Bingleys? Are you concerned about my age? Do you still consider me too young to be out in society?"

"You *are* far too young to be out in society. However, that fact has nothing to do with my belief that now is not the time for you to travel to Hertfordshire."

"You are unfair, Brother."

"Georgiana, you have never expressed an interest in traveling with me before. What is the reason for your sudden change of heart?"

"Well, as you may or may not know, Miss Bingley and I have grown rather fond of each other of late, and she thinks this trip would provide the perfect excuse for me to get better acquainted with her brother."

Darcy drew a quick breath. "Does she now?"

"You need not pretend the thought of an alliance between me and your friend, Mr. Bingley, has not crossed your mind. Do you deny it?"

Frankly, Darcy had no wish to deny it. Neither did he wish to confirm it. His young sister was only six and ten—far too young to entertain thoughts of marriage. He held firmly to that view, despite having interceded on her behalf some time earlier to prevent her from eloping with the one man in the world whom Darcy thought of as his worst enemy: George Wickham.

He knew how much the discovery that Wickham's primary motive in the scheme was her dowry of thirty thousand pounds had pained his young sister. He even feared that suffering a broken heart owing to her disappointed hopes at such a tender age might color her views on marriage.

What a shock it was to learn that she had put that part of her past behind so soon and subsequently transferred her girlish hopes and dreams to his friend Charles Bingley.

"I will only say that Miss Bingley ought not to place the burden of an alliance between our families, which she so desperately covets, on your shoulders. You are far too young to find yourself in such a position."

"Marriage at sixteen is certainly not out of the question. Indeed, it happens all the time."

"Perhaps for young ladies who are far beneath you in consequence. So long as it is within my power to prevent it, no sister of mine shall suffer such a weighty burden. There will be time enough for all that after you have enjoyed a Season or two."

"By my calculation that might be two or three years hence, at most. By then I may have lost my chance to garner Mr. Bingley's affections. Miss

Bingley often says her brother is of an age where he is always making new acquaintances everywhere he goes. Desperate young ladies and their eager mamas who are constantly in search of single young men with large fortunes whom they naturally suspect are in want of wives abound."

He arched his brow. "If engaging in such intercourse defines the nature of your association, I think you and your new friend, Miss Bingley, are spending far too much time in each other's company. It is all the more reason why I do not believe it is a good idea for you to accompany us to Hertfordshire."

"And this is your real opinion—this is your final word."

"It is."

"Very well, but mind you, I like Mr. Bingley, and I suspect he likes me too. I will not be dissuaded in my quest to become Mrs. Charles Bingley someday."

"So long as someday is several years in the making, I shall have no cause to repine."

"It is good to know that I have your blessing." With that Georgiana stood in preparation to quit the room. "Good day, Brother."

"Where are you going?"

"I think I should like to call on Miss Bingley this morning. Who is to say how long she and I will be separated what with your upcoming departure for Hertfordshire? Perchance, I shall see her brother as well. I shall be happy to convey any message to him that you might wish."

"You will remember to ask Mrs. Annesley to join you I trust, and you will remain in her company at all times."

Mrs. Annesley had been employed by Darcy to be his sister's companion in the aftermath of the discovery that her former companion, a Mrs. Younge, had been complicit in the Wickham debacle at Ramsgate. In subjecting Mrs. Annesley to a thorough investigation before hiring her, Darcy intended never to make such a mistake again. His sister meant everything to him.

"Indeed. I would never dream of doing otherwise."

The young lady was gone directly, leaving her brother alone with his thoughts.

Still a bit taken aback by the candid discussion with a sister more than a decade his junior, Darcy sat at his desk, barely attending to the mounds of paperwork he needed to get through in preparation for his upcoming trip.

I have no one to blame other than myself for Georgiana's belief that an alliance between Bingley and her would meet with my approval.

Indeed. Miss Bingley had given the strongest hints of how favorable such an alliance might prove to be. As it was on the heels of Georgiana's thwarted elopement scheme with George Wickham, his former friend and current nemesis, Darcy had said nothing to dampen the young lady's enthusiasm. At the time, he was more concerned about how London society might react should his young sister's actions be discovered. Her reputation would have been ruined. Surely she did not deserve such a dire fate merely for trusting someone whom she had known all her life and, as a consequence, formed a strong attachment which she mistook for love.

Even now, the notion of a possible alliance between his sister and one of his closest friends comforted Darcy. What better two people for each other, he liked to think.

All in due time, however. All in due time.

CHAPTER 3

HER NEXT RECOLLECTION

The lady of the manor house threw open the door of her older daughters' room and poked her head inside. "You girls must hurry, or we shall arrive at the assembly after all the best gentlemen in the Netherfield party are taken. I can assure you my sister Phillips and her daughter will not be late. Even though Phoebe is not so pretty as you, Jane, and she is not so lively as Lydia, she is pretty enough, and she is certainly lively enough, and I cannot bear the thought of her outshining either of my girls."

A woman of mean understanding, little information, and uncertain temper, when Mrs. Bennet was discontented, she fancied herself nervous. The business of her life was to get her daughters married.

How unfair it was to her to have been saddled with five girls when her sister had been burdened with only one. Her sole consolation was her belief that being the prettier of the two Gardiner girls had garnered her such a fate. Marrying off one daughter was nothing at all in comparison with her own onerous job. Mrs. Bennet would not sit idly by and watch her niece secure a husband before one of her own girls reached the altar.

"We shall come down directly, Mama," Elizabeth called out to her mother, who was by then on her way to her younger daughters' room to hurry them along as well. Elizabeth paused for a moment and admired her sister Jane's reflection in the mirror. "How lovely you are, dearest Jane. I dare say neither Phoebe or Charlotte, nor I, stand a chance of garnering the attention of a single gentleman in attendance at the Meryton assembly this evening."

Jane smiled. "Pray, Lizzy, you are not giving any serious thought to taking part in our cousin's challenge."

"Perhaps not at first, but having caught a glimpse of our new neighbor, I can think of far less diverting ways to pass this evening."

At Mrs. Bennet's adamant insistence, Mr. Bennet had been among the first in their neighborhood to call on Mr. Bingley to welcome the young man to his new home. Bingley, subsequently, had returned Mr. Bennet's kindness by calling on him at Longbourn. His visit met with Mrs. Bennet's utter delight, for she contended the young man had entertained hopes of being admitted to a sight of her daughters, whose beauty was so renowned in that part of the country, he surely had heard as much. Alas, he saw only the father. The ladies were somewhat more fortunate, for they had the advantage of ascertaining from an upper window that he was a handsome young man who wore a blue coat and rode a black horse.

"You sound just like Phoebe," Jane said.

"Now, Jane, surely you cannot deny that the prospect of meeting Mr. Bingley does not intrigue you."

"I am certain he is very agreeable, and I certainly welcome the chance to meet new people."

"As it is all but confirmed that upon his most recent return from town he brought twelve ladies and seven gentlemen with him, you shall have plenty of opportunities."

Jane tilted her head ever so slightly. "The last I heard, his party consisted of only six people from London—his five sisters and a cousin."

"Then let us pray his cousin is also a single young man in want of a wife," said Elizabeth as she went to the bed and retrieved a lovely shawl. "And lest I forget—a handsome one at that. Handsome and exceedingly wealthy."

"Oh, Lizzy, you are incorrigible."

The women of Longbourn arrived at the assembly room just in time to command an advantageous view for the entrance of the Netherfield party. What a stunning entry indeed. So much so that any disappointment over the actual size of the party, which consisted of Mr. Bingley, his two sisters, the husband of the eldest, and another young man, was of little consequence.

Mr. Bingley was good-looking and gentleman-like; he had a pleasant countenance, and easy, unaffected manners. His sisters were fine women, with an air of decided fashion. His brother-in-law, Mr. Hurst, merely looked the gentleman; but his friend Mr. Darcy soon drew the attention of the room by his fine, tall person, handsome features and noble mien.

What a fine figure of a man.

"I declare he is much more handsome than Mr. Bingley," cried Phoebe, who was standing next to her cousins and their friend Charlotte.

Speaking in a more hushed voice, the latter said, "He is also said to have ten thousand a year."

"Ten thousand pounds a year!" Phoebe exclaimed with energy.

Charlotte nodded. "And very likely more. He hails from Derbyshire and is said to own half the county."

"How do you know all of this, dearest Charlotte?" Elizabeth inquired.

"Why, my father called on Mr. Bingley this morning."

"Ten thousand a year and half the county," Phoebe repeated with excitement. "Ladies, I think I have found my future husband."

Elizabeth laughed a little at her cousin's conjecture. "Did you hear that, Jane? Our cousin has set her cap on Mr. Bingley's friend, which means Mr. Bingley is quite safe for you."

"And what about you, Cousin Lizzy? Have you no interest in claiming Mr. Bingley for yourself?" After a moment, she gasped. "Surely you do not mean to pursue *my* Mr. Darcy!"

Before Elizabeth could fashion a fitting reply, Mrs. Bennet grabbed both her daughters by the hand and proceeded to coax them to the part of the room where the members of the Netherfield party were standing. Charlotte and Phoebe followed suit.

The introductions were made by Charlotte's father, Sir William Lucas, a friendly, accommodating man whose elevated rank obliged him to attend to such tasks. As a consequence of having to wait for her turn, Elizabeth was able to judge the newcomers with some degree of impunity.

Mr. Bingley was even more handsome from this vantage point. His sisters were fine-looking women, as well. Elizabeth could tell right away that the two ladies thought rather highly of themselves. Their manners were not nearly so easy and unaffected as were Mr. Bingley's.

His brother-in-law, Mr. Hurst, was well-dressed but somewhat disinterested.

And then there was Bingley's friend, Mr. Darcy. Elizabeth did not like to stare, but it was almost impossible not to stare at a gentleman so abundantly endowed with all the best parts of beauty.

My cousin is correct. Mr. Darcy is so much more handsome than Mr. Bingley.

His voice was so deep, so melodic and even sensuous that Elizabeth almost did not notice his haughty air. Almost. Her cousin, in her eagerness to meet the gentleman, stole Elizabeth's place in line at the last moment and offered her hand to the gentleman.

His dark, brooding eyes grew even more foreboding as he reluctantly accepted it and bowed almost imperceptibly.

How rude!

True, her cousin's display could almost be described as vulgar, but surely the gentleman was no stranger to such a reception from an eager young girl.

Not that young Phoebe was put off by Mr. Darcy's cold reception. She merely drifted away as though she had touched the hand of Adonis himself.

It was then Elizabeth's turn to meet everyone.

The bright smile she bestowed upon his friend Bingley and even the polite smile she bestowed upon Bingley's sisters, she promptly dropped when she stood before Mr. Darcy.

She dared not look into his eyes and risk seeing that same haughty stare he bestowed upon her cousin. But then he reached out his hand to her.

"Miss Elizabeth," he said.

Against her will, she looked up. Her eyes met his. He stole her breath away.

Her hand reached out to his, and for a time, Elizabeth forgot what she was about. Her next recollection was of her standing alone on the outside balcony—the same hand against her chest, reminding herself to breathe.

CHAPTER 4

LIVELY AND UNRESERVED

*A*ll in all, the evening passed pleasantly for all parties concerned. That Charlotte, Phoebe, Jane, and Elizabeth should meet to talk about the assembly was absolutely necessary, and the next morning brought the former two to Longbourn to hear and to communicate and, better still, to devise a plan of attack, however reluctant one or more of their party might profess to be.

"Although all four of us can boast of having danced with the amiable Mr. Bingley at the assembly, I do believe it is you, Jane, who has the advantage when it comes to garnering his affections," said Phoebe, clutching one of the decorative pillows from atop her cousin's bed to her chest.

Indeed, having quickly made the acquaintance of all the principal people in the room, the young man proved himself to be very lively and unreserved.

"If I recall correctly Mr. Bingley danced every dance. I do not know that any young lady in the room did not have the pleasure of standing opposite him," Jane said.

"However, you are the only young lady whom he danced with twice. Surely that must count for something," said Charlotte.

Jane ought to have grown used to being the recipient of such accolades. Mrs. Bennet had been absolutely delighted to see her eldest daughter so much admired by the handsome gentleman, as everyone within hearing distance of her at the assembly would attest.

"Jane," said Charlotte, "you need not be so cautious as regards the gentleman. There are only the four of us here after all. Pray, what is your opinion of Mr. Bingley?"

"He is just what a young man ought to be," replied Jane. "He is sensible and good-humored.

He is lively, and I never saw such happy manners!"

"Pray do not neglect to mention the ease with which he recommends himself to strangers," Charlotte said.

"He is also handsome," replied Elizabeth, "which I believe we all agreed a young man ought likewise to be if he possibly can. His character is thereby complete."

"If you do not mind my saying, dear Eliza, aside from his exceedingly good looks, Mr. Darcy's character is decidedly different from his friend's," said Charlotte.

Trying her best to suppress her stomach's fluttering as a consequence of the mentioning of the gentleman's name, Elizabeth asked, "Why in heavens would I mind?"

Why indeed? She would have to be blind not to have noticed the manner in which Mr. Darcy comported himself. The gentleman danced only once with Mrs. Hurst and once with Miss Bingley and spent the rest of the evening walking about the room, occasionally speaking to one of his own party. On more than one occasion, she espied him deliberately turning and walking in the opposite direction when her cousin had attempted to place herself in his path. By the end of the evening, Elizabeth's opinion of the gentleman from Derbyshire was as firmly determined as most of her acquaintances. He was deemed haughty and above his company.

"Do you truly need to ask?"

Elizabeth felt the color spread over her body. Charlotte, after all, had been standing next to her when she was introduced to the gentleman.

Phoebe said, "Yes, Charlotte, why would Lizzy be bothered by anything you have to say about *my* Mr. Darcy?"

"*Your* Mr. Darcy? I would imagine Eliza has something to say about that, do you not, my friend?"

Waving off her intimate friend's concern, Elizabeth said, "On the contrary. Fair is fair, and if I recall correctly, Phoebe did claim him first."

Phoebe nodded contentedly. "So, it is quite decided. Jane shall marry Mr. Bingley, and I shall marry Mr. Darcy. As for the two of you—"

"Pray, do not concern yourself with my marital prospects," cried Charlotte.

"I concur," Elizabeth replied.

"But all four of us were meant to find

husbands during the course of a twelvemonth. Whatever shall the two of you do?"

Elizabeth said, "I rather suppose someone will happen along. Perhaps Mr. Bingley and Mr. Darcy both have cousins."

Meanwhile, the conversation taking place three miles away in the drawing room at Netherfield had taken on a rather different tone.

"I never met so many pretty women in one place in all my life," said Charles Bingley.

"Were we even at the same assembly?" cried his younger sister, Caroline. "For my part, I never witnessed such a shabby gathering of single females desperately in want of husbands in one place. Do you not agree, Mr. Darcy?"

"I dare say there were more than a few young ladies who might best be described as tolerable. None of them were handsome enough to tempt me."

"I did notice you walking about looking rather stupid for the better part of the evening," Charles declared. "Refusing to dance with anyone other than my sisters. I should not be so fastidious as you for a kingdom."

"You might try a bit of fastidiousness from time to time. It might very well spare you a great deal of trouble."

"I am sure I do not take your meaning."

"Think about it, Charles," his elder sister, Mrs. Louisa Hurst, replied. "Did you not single out Miss Bennet for two dances? Can you even begin to imagine what her family and friends are now thinking? No doubt Mrs. Bennet is planning a wedding here at Netherfield as we speak."

"What man would not be proud to find himself engaged to marry Miss Bennet?" Charles inquired with the utmost sincerity. "She is the most beautiful creature I ever beheld. Surely you agree, Darcy."

"Frankly, Bingley, I am unable to account for all the women you have ever beheld or how they rank in beauty. Miss Bennet is very pretty; however, she smiles too much."

"And what is your assessment of her sister Miss Elizabeth, who is next to her in age?"

"Surely you cannot expect me to give an accounting of every young woman in attendance," Darcy said, his voice signaling his annoyance.

"Well, not every woman—just this particular woman. I could not help noticing the manner in which you greeted her."

Before Darcy could fashion a response, Caroline began voicing her own opinion of Miss Elizabeth Bennet and in a manner that was less than flattering. It was just as well, for this gave Darcy time to reflect on precisely what his reaction to seeing her had been.

In a word—bewitched.

His telling reaction to the beguiling young woman had played a large part in his subsequent behavior the evening before. He was far too busy rebuking himself to worry what Bingley's new neighbors thought of him. Men of his stature did not give consideration to the daughters of a country gentleman who were so far beneath him in consequence as to be deemed laughable.

It simply is not done.

CHAPTER 5

SOME MISHAP

A FORTNIGHT HENCE...

"Pray, remind me again of the reason you wished to invite Miss Bennet to dine with us, dear Caroline."

"After we called on the Bennets at Longbourn, I am certain her eager mama would feel obliged to return the honor. If I am forced to spend time in the company of our brother's new neighbors, I would much rather subject myself to the eldest daughter's presence. I find the others absolutely dreadful. Why, between the mother and that impertinent Miss Eliza, I do not know which I prefer less. As for the younger three, I would rather go mad than be forced to endure their mundane dribble and childish antics."

"Heavens, you are entirely too severe on our brother's neighbors." Louisa waited for a rebuttal from her sister in her own defense. Having received no such denial of her ill-opinion of the ladies of Longbourn, she said, "I do have to wonder about your seeming tolerance of Miss Bennet, however."

"What do you mean? Did we not agree that Miss Bennet is a dear girl?"

"We did, but surely you have noticed how Charles dotes on her."

Indeed, since the assembly at Meryton where their brother had danced two sets with Miss Bennet, there had been at least four other incidences of his dining with her in company as well as seeing her at his own home once.

"Have you no concern at all how his admiration for Miss Bennet might impact your favorite wish for an alliance between him and Miss Georgiana Darcy? Or shall I say your second favorite wish? For what could matter more than your ardent wish to become the next mistress of Pemberley?"

What woman of sound mind did not wish for such a distinction? Caroline silently considered. Pemberley was not an inconsequential place, and certainly, its master was not an inconsequential man. To be the mistress of such a place and thereby the wife of such a man, must truly be something. Every woman she met, she deemed a competitor in one way or another. If there was but one exception, it was Miss Bennet. No—that young woman seemed more interested in Charles Bingley as evidenced by her abundance of smiles directed at him whenever they were together. Knowing her brother as well as she did, Caroline almost pitied Miss Bennet.

"Louisa," Caroline responded, "you and I both know how our brother is wont to fall in love with every angel he meets. There is no reason in the world for me to suppose this time will be any different."

"Ah, but what if this time is the exception? There is always a first time, you know."

"That is precisely why I invited Miss Bennet to join us this afternoon. There is no chance of our brother being tempted by her lovely smiles, for lest you forget, Charles along with Mr. Darcy and Hurst are dining with the officers. Jane

Bennet will be away from Netherfield long before they are expected to return."

"Caroline, you do think of everything."

"I try to," she replied. Consulting the mantel clock, she cried, "Where in heavens is she?"

Louisa glanced outside a nearby window. "The weather appears to be taking a terrible turn for the worse. I suppose she may have changed her mind and decided not to join us."

Rolling her eyes, the younger woman was not nearly so charitable as the elder. "With such a mother as Mrs. Bennet, I dare say the possibility that she would allow her daughter to forgo the opportunity to ingratiate herself with the sisters of a gentleman so rich as Charles is little to none," Caroline mocked.

Caroline had hardly finished her snide speech when the drawing room doors were opened and in walked the butler.

"Miss Bennet," he said, bowing. There stood Jane, dwarfed by the towering man's presence, and dripping wet from head to toes.

The Bingley sisters' mouths gaped. "Miss Bennet," cried Caroline. "Pray, what on earth happened to you?"

Abandoning her sewing, the elder sister

hurried across the room to where Jane stood. Her voice filled with concern, she asked, "Was there some mishap with your carriage? Were you forced to travel the rest of the way by foot?"

Caroline had also come to Jane's side, but at a less urgent pace.

Jane shook her head. "No—" Covering her mouth with her gloved hand, she began sneezing. "I—" She sneezed again. "I came here on horseback," she explained before giving in to an unavoidable bout of sneezes.

"Horseback!" Louisa and Caroline cried in unison.

"What were you thinking?" Caroline asked.

"What does it matter at this point?" Louisa asked. "Come, Miss Bennet, we must see that you remove your wet clothing before you catch your death of cold."

The three ladies were quickly on their way up the stairs, the elder clearly concerned for the guest's well-being, and the younger, no doubt, puzzled by the guest's sensibility.

"Horseback," she silently mouthed for her sister's benefit alone, "are these people too poor to afford a carriage?" Both sisters merely shrugged.

The Bingley sisters were considerate enough

to remain by Jane's side until she was settled comfortably in a nice, warm bed in one of the guest apartments.

Concerned about a gradual turn toward the worse in Jane's condition as the evening progressed, the decision was made to have Mr. Jones, the local apothecary from Meryton, come and examine Jane early the next morning.

The gentleman's prognosis upon examining the sick lady was met with a mixture of relief and trepidation on the part of the two sisters: relief that Jane suffered a cold and nothing graver, and trepidation because Jane was commanded to remain in bed at Netherfield for several days so as not to risk a worsening of her condition.

"Several days!" cried Caroline to Louisa once Mr. Jones was gone and the ladies were at liberty to speak in private. "I dare say Netherfield will be overrun by Bennets before we know. How on earth are we to endure?"

CHAPTER 6

SIGHT TO BEHOLD

*D*esperation accompanied Elizabeth on her solitary journey that morning. Earlier, she had received a letter from her sister Jane, who had fallen ill while visiting her friends at Netherfield Park.

The words in Jane's letter, though meant to be reassuring, had failed miserably in easing Elizabeth's distress upon reading them.

"My dearest Lizzy," the letter had begun, "I find myself very unwell this morning, which, I suppose, is to be imputed to my getting wet through yesterday. My kind friends will not hear of my returning till I am better. They also insisted on my seeing Mr. Jones. Therefore, I implore you, do not be alarmed if you should hear of his having been to me. I believe it a bit much, for excepting a sore throat and headache, there is not much the matter with me. — Yours, etc."

Elizabeth knew her sister too well not to be concerned. *Jane is too good to complain about anything, even her own health. My sister needs me.*

Elizabeth's steps grew even more impatient. *What was my mother thinking in insisting that Jane travel from Longbourn to Netherfield on horseback when the skies above threatened a torrential downpour?*

Of course, Elizabeth knew precisely what her mother was thinking. She had meant to play matchmaker between Jane and Mr. Bingley knowing full well that Jane would be forced to stay the night should the weather prognostication hold true.

Having navigated any number of hills and stiles successfully, Elizabeth underestimated the width of a puddle in her path. She jumped. But she did not jump far enough, and instead of landing on her feet, she found herself lying flat on her back—her bonnet, her spencer, her gown, her everything covered in mud. What a wretched sight to behold.

How shall I possibly arrive at Netherfield looking like

this? Even Jane might find my appearance objectionable, and Jane never thinks badly of anyone.

The sound of approaching horse hooves caught her wholly unaware, and before she knew what she was about, Elizabeth was staring up into the eyes of the last person she wished to see.

Giving no mind to what his own appearance would be, the gentleman quickly dismounted and extended his gloved hand. "Miss Elizabeth," he said, "are you quite all right?"

Before Elizabeth could reply, he said, "Take my hand."

Without hesitation, she did exactly as she was told, although she did not like finding herself in such a position one bit. After all, she was not one of those helpless females she often read about in romance novels. She was quite sure that she could manage quite well on her own had he not come along when he did. Once she was standing upright, albeit drenched in mud, she told him as much.

"That may very well be, but I am here, and thus I am obliged to see that you arrive at your intended destination safely. I presume you are on your way to Netherfield to attend your ailing sister."

She nodded. "I am."

"Pray you will not misunderstand what I am about to say, but—"

"Mr. Darcy, if you really feel it necessary to couch whatever you intend to say in such terms as that, perhaps you ought not to say it at all."

"Oh, but I feel I must."

"Pray allow me to guess. You find the idea of my arriving at your friend's home in such a dreadful state as this completely intolerable."

"Actually, what I was about to say is you must allow me to carry you there on horseback in order to hasten your safe arrival, so that you may quickly remove your wet clothing. There is no need for two Bennet daughters to convalesce at Netherfield."

Elizabeth wrapped her arms about her shoulders to ward off a slight chill. "Should I accept your offer of assistance, I am not certain which would be the greater scandal: my arrival in such a state of disarray or my arriving on horseback with you."

Darcy threw off his greatcoat and wrapped it about Elizabeth's shoulders. Once again Elizabeth found herself peering into his dark, brooding eyes. And they were standing so close. Fortunately for her or not so fortunately, an untidy strand of hair fell down her face. Removing his glove, Darcy brushed the errand lock aside.

Her reaction to his nearness was as puzzling as it had been upon first meeting him at the assembly.

What is it about this man that baffles me so?

Whatever it was, she had spent the past weeks whenever in company with him trying her best not to find out. Not that the gentleman meant to make it easy. Rarely did Elizabeth accidentally glance Mr. Darcy's way and not find him looking at her. Indeed, in much the same way as he was looking at her that very moment.

He is proud and above his company, Elizabeth reminded herself in one breath. *He is the most handsome man my eyes have ever beheld,* she silently considered in the next.

"I shall accompany you into the manor house completely undetected by the rest of the party, and once you have donned fresh clothing, you may visit your sister."

Elizabeth swallowed. "Your plan lacks one critical element, sir."

"If you are speaking of attire, I am thinking you can dispatch a note to Longbourn to have a change of clothing sent to you at Netherfield. What say you to the scheme, Miss Elizabeth? Mind you, I have no intention of leaving you stranded in your present state. Either I shall accompany you to Netherfield or I shall accompany you to Longbourn. The choice is entirely up to you."

Elizabeth was bound and determined to visit her sister. A return to Longbourn might very well delay her for hours perhaps an entire day. There really was only one thing to do. "I shall place myself in your hands, Mr. Darcy."

True to his word, Mr. Darcy aided Elizabeth in entering the manor house undetected by any of the Bingleys.

When they arrived at the top of the stairs, Elizabeth said, "If you will tell me which room my sister is in, I believe I shall no longer be in need of your assistance, Mr. Darcy."

"Your sister's apartment is just down the hallway—directly across from mine, in fact. We are almost there. Come."

"No!" Elizabeth cried with more urgency than

she had intended. She had almost forgotten she was still draped by the gentleman's coat. Savoring the fresh masculine scent of this man who was very much a stranger, she slowly removed the coat and handed it over to him. "That is to say, you have done more than enough, sir. I am in your debt."

Her clothes were no more presentable now than when he had aided her to her feet when they were on the lane.

"What of your plan to send for a change of clothing from Longbourn?" Mr. Darcy inquired, referring to their conversation while she rode atop his stead and he walked along, guiding the horse's reins. "Shall I show you to an unoccupied apartment, so you might address those matters first?"

"No!" Elizabeth cried once more. "I believe I may attend to all that once I am inside my sister's room." Here, she felt the color spread all over her body. She was sure he was not judging her—not after having attended her so diligently in escorting her there. However, there was something about the way he looked at her that gave her pause.

His look was not unlike the look he bestowed when they were introduced at the assembly—a look that caused her to suffer such sentiments she was sure she would never forget.

By now they had resumed walking down the long hallway, their footsteps muted by the rich carpeting beneath their feet, past any number of closed doors and walls of exquisite tapestry. Each step made her more and more aware of her appearance. Her companion, by comparison, looked as though he had stepped from a painting.

At length, she asked, "How much farther, sir?"

He stopped. "We are here. Your sister's apartment," he said, his hand gesturing accordingly.

Against her will, Elizabeth threw a quick glance to the opposite side of the hallway.

"My apartment," he said, nodding ever so slightly. "Pray you will let me know if I can be of further service, Miss Elizabeth."

Their eyes met—both holding each other's gaze for a moment or two. Her whole body trembled under the weight of his stare, or perhaps her damp clothes were the cause. More likely, a little of both.

"I shall," Elizabeth said, tentatively. Turning, she placed her hand on the doorknob of Jane's apartment. She tapped lightly with her other hand before opening the door and slipping inside.

Before shutting the door completely, Elizabeth looked back.

Mr. Darcy was still standing there. Looking into his eyes once more, almost searching them, Elizabeth smiled a little. And then, she closed the door.

CHAPTER 7

CONSIDERATION IN THE WORLD

Not very long after that, Elizabeth sat beside her sister and pressed a moist towel against Jane's forehead. Jane slowly awakened. "Dearest Lizzy, thank you for coming to see me."

"There is nothing on this earth that would have prevented my being here."

"Have I been asleep for very long? How long have you been here?"

"Pray, dearest Jane, do not worry yourself with any of that. I am here now, and I will remain here with you for so long as it takes."

At that moment, the Bingley sisters crept into the room. "Why, Miss Eliza," the younger woman cried, "When in heavens did you arrive?"

Elizabeth said, "It is very nice to see you too, Miss Bingley ... Mrs. Hurst. Allow me to thank you for taking such prodigious care of my sister."

"Oh, but it is the least we can do. Miss Bennet is such a favorite of ours." Turning to her older sister, Miss Bingley said, "Is she not, dearest Louisa?"

Twisting a strand of pearls draped around her neck, the other lady nodded. "She is indeed. It is our pleasure to have her. It is a shame the circumstances for her being here are such as they are, but we are determined to make the best of things." She walked closer to Jane's bedside. "How are you feeling, my dear?"

Her voice rather weak, Jane said, "I am feeling so much better now that my sister is here."

"Capital. And you need not worry one bit, for your sister is welcome to remain here for so long as necessary to be of comfort to you while you recover. Caroline and I will do all that is within our power to make certain Miss Elizabeth feels just as welcomed as you. Is that not correct, Caroline?"

"Oh, indeed. It really is a shame that all the Bennet daughters have not arrived at our doorstep. What a lively party we would be."

At five o'clock the two ladies retired to dress for dinner. Elizabeth was summoned at half-past six to join them in the dining room. With some reluctance on her part, Elizabeth left her sister's side and proceeded down the long hallway—her only consolation being the chance to be once again in Mr. Darcy's company.

For the past few hours or so, any thoughts she had that did not center on her sister's wellbeing dwelt solely on Mr. Darcy and how kind he had been to her earlier that day. She was beginning to suspect he was nothing at all as she had thought.

He is not haughty—indeed, I believe he is rather shy.

The ensuing moments belied her tender sentiments. As she descended the grand staircase, her presence went unnoticed, thus affording the chance for Elizabeth to hear a rather lively discussion unfolding between certain members of the Netherfield party as they proceeded to the dining room.

She might have cleared her throat or engaged in some other scheme to make her presence known, and she would have except for the fact that she was a very curious creature by nature and especially when she was at the center of what was being discussed.

"Her manners are appalling. Indeed, a mixture of pride and impertinence; she has no conversation, no style, no beauty," Louisa declared.

"She has nothing, in short, to recommend her, but being an excellent walker—that is if one is to be expected to believe she walked all the way here from her father's estate—unchaperoned no less and in such dreadful weather as this," added Caroline.

"One can only imagine how she must have looked upon her arrival."

"No doubt wild-eyed with unkempt, blowsy hair and her petticoat, six inches deep in mud, I am absolutely certain. Is there any wonder she sent home for a change of attire before any of us were the wiser?"

"How very nonsensical to come at all! Why must she be scampering about the country because her sister has a cold?" Louisa asked.

"To walk three miles, or four miles, or five miles, or whatever it is, and alone, quite alone! What could she mean by it? It seems to me to show an abominable sort of conceited independence, a most country-town indifference to decorum," Caroline concluded.

"It shows an affection for her sister that is very pleasing," said Bingley.

"A rather odd sort of affection, if you ask me. I have an excessive regard for Miss Jane Bennet, she is really a very sweet girl, and I wish with all my heart she were well settled. But with such a father and mother, and such low connections, I am afraid there is no chance of it," said the younger woman.

"I think I have heard you say that their uncle is an attorney in Meryton."

"Yes; and they have another, who lives somewhere near Cheapside."

"That is capital," added her sister, and they both laughed heartily.

"If they had uncles enough to fill all of Cheapside," cried Bingley, "it would not make them one jot less agreeable."

"But it must very materially lessen their chance of marrying men of any consideration in the world," replied Darcy.

Hearing this, Elizabeth could no longer help but be affected.

And this is his real opinion, she silently affirmed.

This is who Mr. Darcy really is! This is what he thinks of people whom he perceives as lesser than himself in consequence.

At that moment, Miss Bingley threw a casual glance over her shoulder and saw Elizabeth was not very far behind their party. She stopped and waited for Netherfield's newest guest, encouraging everyone else to do so as well.

"Why, Miss Eliza, I wonder that you did not make your presence known. We are such an intimate party, but that is no excuse for neglecting you."

"On the contrary, Miss Bingley," Elizabeth said, now standing directly beside the others. "I do not feel neglected in the least bit." She then looked squarely at Mr. Darcy. "You must not give such thoughts any consideration in the world."

Darcy knew he should have been more circumspect when speaking of the Bennet daughters' marital prospects earlier that evening. Miss Bingley, with her acerbic wit, always knew precisely what to say to bring out the worst in people which was precisely the reason he did not like the idea of his younger sister being unduly influenced by her.

Were he to judge by Miss Elizabeth's chilly reception toward him for the remainder of the evening, he was confident that she had heard him speak as he had. He would apologize to her if it were not for the fact that he had spoken nothing but the truth.

Admittedly, he knew nothing at all about the Bennet daughters of Longbourn—the size of their fortune or lack thereof, or even their connections. Their being so intimately connected with people in trade by way of their mother being a tradesman's daughter and her two brothers, one a merchant in town who lived near his warehouses and the other a lawyer in the nearby town of Meryton was all he needed to know.

Miss Elizabeth's situation in life did not, indeed could not, keep thoughts of her from accompanying him to sleep that night, however.

A most satisfying slumber had not been long in the making before Mr. Darcy knew everything a man of sense and education with knowledge of the world could ever wish to know about a woman: the touch of her lips pressed tenderly against his, the tantalizing taste of her, the feel of her in his arms, the warmth of her body next to his—her softness and his hardness as one.

What must have been hours later, he bolted up in bed and shook his head. He released a deep sigh of relief.

I was only dreaming. This realization drifted from relief to regret and just as quickly as that, to consolation, for so much as he realized it was wrong to think of an innocent young woman in such a manner—a young woman who could never mean anything to him owing to her station in life in comparison to his own, he could certainly enjoy her charming wit and bewitching dark eyes by day and dream of cherishing her with her oh so pleasing figure and tantalizing lips by night for so long as he remained in Hertfordshire.

So long as I do nothing that might raise Miss Elizabeth's expectations, what is the harm in admiring her from afar?

CHAPTER 8

AN OBVIOUS PLOY

*T*hough the events of the previous evening had thoroughly cemented Elizabeth's opinion of the members of the Netherfield party—each of them in their turn, she felt it absolutely necessary to acknowledge the Bingleys' benevolence towards Jane by accepting the invitation to dine with them in the breakfast room.

She now knew and understood the younger woman was nowhere nearly so delighted by her presence as was her brother, Mr. Bingley, which made being there all the more uncomfortable, albeit oddly satisfying. However, nothing could have prepared Elizabeth for what happened just as their party adjourned to the drawing room. A footman formally attired in livery more suited to a king's servant entered the room.

"A Miss Phoebe Phillips," he declared. Seconds later, Elizabeth's cousin waltzed into the room, adorned in a light blue muslin gown, a dark blue spencer, and a lovely bonnet which Elizabeth knew to be recently purchased.

"Phoebe, what on earth are you doing here?" Elizabeth could not help but exclaim.

"My question exactly!" Miss Bingley uttered.

After acknowledging each of the occupants of the room with a slight curtsy, and no doubt disappointed by Mr. Darcy's absence, Phoebe said, "Why, Cousin Lizzy, you know how fond I am of my dear, dear cousin Jane. Why, I simply could not sleep a wink until I saw firsthand how she is getting along. One can never take anything for granted where these things are concerned. Even a trifling cold has the possibility of taking a turn for the worse."

"How fortunate Miss Bennet is indeed to have such thoughtful relations," declared the older Bingley sister.

"Thoughtful indeed, and for my part, any relation of Miss Bennet's is welcome in my home," said Mr. Bingley, smiling in abundance.

"One might be careful what one wishes for, dear brother," said Miss Bingley, throwing her sister a knowing look.

"For now, I wish for nothing more than Miss Bennet's complete recovery, which is sure to transpire in the company of caring relations and friends alike."

The Bingleys carried on in that manner for a while, and when she could, Phoebe took her cousin aside. "I suppose you think you are very clever, Miss Lizzy."

"Whatever do you mean by that?"

"You know very well what I mean."

"No—I am afraid I do not, but I am sure that will not prevent you from telling me."

"You may pretend to be ignorant, but I for one am not fooled. I know your mother contrived to have Jane thrown into Mr. Bingley's path because she boasted of having done so to my mother."

"And what can any of that have to do with me?"

"It is one thing for your mother to behave as she did, for it is very much in keeping with the rules of the game, but for you to throw yourself into Mr. Darcy's path in such an egregious manner is beyond the pale. You know you are not playing fairly. I claimed Mr. Darcy!"

Somewhat aggrieved, Elizabeth said, "You do know that you are the only one of the four of us who gives a fig about your twelve-month matrimonial challenge, do you not?"

"What else would one expect you to say, given your flagrant disregard for my feelings?"

"Phoebe, this is neither the time nor the place to be entertaining such a discussion. My sister is very ill. I am here for one purpose, and that is to be by her side. Now, either you came all this way to see her or you simply used my sister's illness as a ploy to be near *your* Mr. Darcy. If the first, then I am more than happy to accompany you to Jane's room. If the latter, then I shall leave you to your own devices in garnering his attention. At this point, either of your choices can have no effect on me."

Upon observing a young lady entering the library, Darcy closed his book and stood, intending to quit the room. To his chagrin, the young lady hurried in his direction and stopped directly before him.

She stood closer than the extent of their acquaintance warranted, prompting Darcy to ease a step back.

"Do you not remember meeting me, Mr. Darcy?"

The young lady was comely enough for Darcy to recall having seen her before, but not enough for him to recall with any specificity where that might have taken place.

"To be frank, I have been introduced to countless young ladies such as yourself since my arrival here in Hertfordshire. Perhaps you might do me the honor of refreshing my memory."

Phoebe held out her hand. "I am Miss Phillips—Miss Phoebe Phillips."

Mr. Darcy accepted the young lady's proffered hand, bowed slightly, and released it promptly. "It is a pleasure to make your acquaintance." It was the polite thing to say after all. He had no desire to be rude to one of his friend's guests. On the other hand, he did not mean to encourage her either. Engaging the affections of young ladies of lesser means was just the kind of thing he avoided doing.

The irony was not lost on Darcy what with his resolve to admire Miss Elizabeth Bennet in secret.

He simply could not help himself for the beguiling young woman was unlike any woman he had ever met, with her amazing eyes and her charming wit.

This young lady is no Miss Elizabeth Bennet.

His purpose in being in the library was the possibility that she might wander in during the course of the morning.

"The pleasure is entirely mine, I assure you," Darcy heard the young lady standing before him reply in a coquettish manner.

As though realizing the perils of spending time alone in the library with the young lady suddenly dawned on him, Darcy said, "Miss Phillips, pray you will excuse me. I have urgent business to attend elsewhere."

Phoebe pouted a little. "Oh, but I only just arrived. What is more, it is as though fate conspired to place the two of us in each other's path."

"I beg your pardon?"

"You see, sir, I am in need of your assistance in locating a book to read to my cousin Jane, and well, I thought you might help me find the perfect one."

"Your cousin? So, you are Miss Elizabeth's cousin."

Batting her eyelashes, Phoebe nodded. "I am. Has she mentioned me to you?"

He shrugged. His countenance a bit puzzled, he said, "No. I am afraid she has not."

"Oh! And I was so sure that she would have in view of the circumstances."

"Circumstances? What circumstances, Miss Phillips?"

Phoebe nearly gasped. "Oh! Do not mind all that, sir. There will be time enough for such matters at a later date and perhaps a different place. For now, I really must beg for your assistance in locating the perfect book for dear Jane."

Darcy had too much experience with young ladies of Miss Phillips' ilk to be affected by such an obvious ploy. "As you know your cousin Miss Bennet far better than I might ever expect to know her, I must insist you pardon me, for I am certain I would only impede your success."

"I rather disagree. In fact, I have a fair knowledge of the books in this library, having visited Netherfield on more than one occasion before it was let by your friend Mr. Bingley. I believe the perfect book is just over there." Phoebe walked swiftly to the stacks and scurried up the ladder. Her boldness seemed to ebb when she reached one of its higher rungs.

"Oh! Mr. Darcy," she cried. "I do not know what has come over me. Why—I completely forgot I am deathly afraid of heights."

"Stay where you are," Darcy declared before proceeding to walk across the room in the opposite direction.

Seeing this, Phoebe exclaimed. "Sir, I need your help. Pray, where are you going?"

"To summon a footman, of course." After doing just that, Darcy said, "There, help is on the way." He bowed. "Good day, Miss Phillips."

Darcy was gone directly.

CHAPTER 9

SUCH A PLEASING MANNER

*F*eeling somewhat put upon, Elizabeth was not sure which vexed her more: her cousin Phoebe's impertinent visit or Elizabeth's mother and sisters' visit the very next day.

All Elizabeth knew was her sister Jane had recovered enough for the two of them to soon be taking their leave of Netherfield. She could hardly wait.

Making matters worse, she had been prevailed upon by her mother's antics to stand up for Mr. Darcy time and again throughout her visit.

In so doing, Elizabeth had inadvertently led Miss Bingley to view her as a rival for Mr. Darcy's attention - an unenviable position indeed considering how Elizabeth felt about the couple and their games of cat and mouse. He had frequently engaged Elizabeth in conversation for the better part of the evening to Miss Bingley's exclusion as well as her dismay. Elizabeth did not like being used in such a manner, and she meant to tell the gentleman how she felt as soon as she had a chance.

The day after Mrs. Bennet's visit proceeded in much the same way as the day before; Mr. Darcy's attention toward Elizabeth did not abate.

After a half hour or so of being chased around the room by Miss Bingley, Mr. Darcy decided to apply to the overzealous young lady and Elizabeth for an indulgence of some music. Miss Bingley moved with some alacrity to the pianoforte. After a polite request that Elizabeth would lead the way, which Elizabeth politely declined, she seated herself.

Mrs. Hurst sang with her sister, and while they were thus employed, Elizabeth could not help observing, as she turned over some music books that lay on the instrument, how frequently Mr. Darcy's eyes were fixed on her. After playing some Italian songs, Miss Bingley varied the charm by a lively Scotch air, and soon enough Mr. Darcy drew near Elizabeth.

"Do not you feel a great inclination, Miss Bennet, to seize such an opportunity of dancing a reel?"

She smiled but made no answer.

As though surprised by her silence, Mr. Darcy repeated the question. "Do not you feel a great inclination, Miss Bennet, to seize such an opportunity of dancing a reel?"

"Oh!" said she, "I heard you before, but I could not immediately determine what to say in reply. You wanted me, I know, to say 'Yes,' that you might have the pleasure of despising my taste; but I always delight in overthrowing those kinds of schemes and cheating a person of their premeditated contempt. I have, therefore, made up my mind to tell you that I do not want to dance a reel at all. Now despise me if you dare."

"Indeed, I do not dare."

The two of them bantered on in this fashion for a time, and its effect on Miss Bingley's performance was undeniable. Abandoning the pianoforte altogether, the young lady hastened to place herself directly between Mr. Darcy and Elizabeth. Welcoming the reprieve, Elizabeth escaped their little group as soon as she could and returned to the solitude of her book. Finding herself between Mr. Darcy and his most ardent admirer, Miss Bingley, was the last thing in the world Elizabeth wished for. Still, she could not help but be entertained by the prospect of Mr. Darcy's anguish. That was until Mr. Darcy managed once again to draw Elizabeth back into the heart of their discussion.

"Miss Elizabeth," he said, "takes an eager interest in reading. I have always considered the constant improvement of one's mind by extensive reading to be the hallmark of an accomplished woman."

Elizabeth wanted to say something—anything to dissuade such a speech, but before she could fashion a fitting response, Miss Bingley cried, "Oh! Reading no doubt has its place, but a truly accomplished woman must possess a certain something in her air and manner of walking, the tone of her voice, her address and expressions. Otherwise, the word will be but half-deserved. And one must not neglect the importance of physical beauty, else the more discerning among us might find an otherwise accomplished woman to be merely tolerable."

"I am given to believe that beauty is in the eyes of the beholder."

"You would say that," said Miss Bingley in a manner which suggested his remark held a broader context known only between the two of them.

How Elizabeth wished both of them would just go away and leave her to her book.

At length, a servant entered the room and handed Miss Bingley a note. Upon reading it, the young woman quit the room in quite a rush. Elizabeth seized the chance to speak to Mr. Darcy with impunity.

"Miss Bingley has left the room, sir."

"I beg your pardon?"

"She is gone now. You no longer need to behave as though I am of any consequence. Your earlier pretense worked."

"Is that how you see me, Miss Elizabeth? As one who would make sport of one young lady merely to disappoint the hopes of another?"

Elizabeth shrugged. "I do not know that I would have stated it so delicately as that, but as the words are your own—"

"Forgive me."

Taken aback by his unexpected declaration, Elizabeth cried, "Pardon me?"

"Forgive me, Miss Elizabeth, if I gave you cause to think my desire to get to know you better was merely a ploy to frustrate Miss Bingley."

"Then, you do not deny that was your intention?"

"I do not deny that frustrating Miss Bingley is not without its own rewards," Mr. Darcy responded, moving closer to Elizabeth, as close to her as he had ever been throughout the entirety of their acquaintance.

How she bewitched him. Gazing into her dark eyes, he added, "However, in spending the greater part of the evening in such a pleasing manner as I did, I believe I was thinking only of you."

CHAPTER 10

THE BEST PARTS OF BEAUTY

Other than the addition of a rather unwelcome guest at Longbourn, a distant cousin and the estate's heir apparent, Mr. William Collins, the days that marked the Bennet sisters' return from Netherfield had been rather uneventful.

Save the middle Bennet daughter, Miss Mary, a most welcome surprise awaited the Bennet girls and their cousin Phoebe that particular day in Meryton when their attention was caught by a young man, whom they had never seen before, of most gentleman-like appearance, walking with another officer on the other side of the way. One was an officer—a Mr. Denny, a favorite of the youngest girls, Kitty and Lydia, who had recently returned from London. He bowed as they passed.

All were struck with the stranger's air, and all wondered who he could be. Determined to find out, Kitty and Lydia led the way across the street, under the pretense of wanting something in an opposite shop. Soon enough, all the young ladies in the party stood face to face with the two gentlemen. Mr. Denny addressed them directly and entreated permission to introduce his friend, Mr. Wickham, who had returned with him the day before from town, and he was happy to say had accepted a commission in their corps.

In the younger sisters' estimation, this was exactly as it should be, for the young man wanted only regimentals to make him completely charming. His appearance was greatly in his favor. He had all the best parts of beauty: a fine countenance, a good figure, and a very pleasing address.

The introduction was followed up on his side by a happy readiness of conversation—a readiness at the same time perfectly correct and unassuming, and the whole party was still standing and talking together very agreeably when the sound of horses drew their notice, and Darcy and Bingley were seen riding down the street.

On distinguishing the ladies of the group, the two gentlemen came directly towards them and began the usual civilities. Bingley was the principal spokesman, and Miss Bennet the primary object. He was then, he said, on his way to Longbourn with the purpose of inquiring after her. Mr. Darcy corroborated his friend's declaration with a bow, and then his eyes were suddenly arrested by the sight of the stranger.

Elizabeth happening to see the countenance of both as they looked at each other, was all astonishment at the effect of the meeting. Both changed color, one looked white, the other red. Mr. Wickham, after a few moments, touched his hat—a salutation which Mr. Darcy just deigned to return.

What could be the meaning of it? It was impossible to imagine. In another minute, Mr. Bingley, without seeming to have noticed what passed, took leave and rode on with his friend.

Seemingly undaunted by Mr. Darcy's puzzling behavior, Phoebe's spirits were lively, although the gentleman had done nothing to stoke her affections. And when the ladies were parted from the pleasant company of Mr. Denny and Mr. Wickham, she pulled Elizabeth away from all the other members of their party.

"Cousin Lizzy," Phoebe said, "is not Mr. Wickham almost everything the ideal husband ought to be?" She clasped her hand to her bosom. "He is tall. He is amiable, and best of all, he is exceedingly handsome."

"Phoebe, do you mean to say after one look at Mr. Wickham, Mr. Darcy has now somehow diminished in your esteem? How fickle you are!"

"Oh, no! You mistake my meaning. I am not suggesting Mr. Wickham is ideal for me. I believe he is the perfect husband for *you*!"

Elizabeth would have been lying if she said Mr. Wickham was not a handsome gentleman. Indeed, he was blessed with all that was pleasing to a lady's eye: impeccable dress, perfect hair, smoldering eyes, and a charismatic smile. She dared not encourage her cousin's whims, and thus she said nothing.

Elizabeth's silence, Phoebe must have considered acquiescence. She said, "Oh, I knew you would agree with me. Is this not divine? Now if only there were a man for our dear Charlotte." After a brief pause to gather her thoughts, she said, "I have a brilliant idea! I know your cousin,

Mr. Collins, is intended for one or the other of either you, Jane, Mary, Kitty, or Lydia, but as you are now safe from him, perhaps we might save your sisters too by throwing him in Charlotte's path."

Elizabeth silently scoffed at her cousin's conjecture. *Given my preference, none of us would be burdened by a proposal of marriage from Mr. Collins. Neither my sisters, nor my dearest Charlotte, and most especially not me.*

Having been compelled to be in his company since she and Jane returned to Longbourn from Netherfield, Elizabeth could rightfully say the man was ridiculous—self-important and sycophantic. Her father had taken her aside on the heels of their first evening with the gentleman to explain his purpose in visiting Longbourn.

"Prepare yourself for something dreadful," Mr. Bennet had advised.

"What could be more dreadful than the prospect of spending time in Mr. Collins's company for the foreseeable future?"

"I received a letter from him not too long ago which goes into some detail about his motives for coming here, or should I say, expectations. Indeed, being fully aware of the hardship to his fair cousins owing to the entail and being cautious of appearing forward and presumptuous, he wanted to assure me that he has come prepared to admire you and your sisters."

A rather odd mixture of quick parts, sarcastic humor, reserve, and caprice, Mr. Bennet had concluded, "I can only imagine which of my daughters will be the happy bride."

"I dare say everyone would be happy with the arrangement," Phoebe continued, recalling Elizabeth to the present. "Our Charlotte wants nothing more than a home of her own, and that, Mr. Collins can surely provide. For Heaven's sake, she might one day be mistress of Longbourn."

Elizabeth's pulse quickened as it often did whenever anyone spoke of the entail on her father's estate—even when spoken in jest. Nothing was more natural than death, but the thought of what her father's passing meant was no laughing matter. Added to her grief would be the loss of everything she held dear. *My mother, my sisters, and I may very well be thrown into the hedgerows.* The irony of her family's situation and her cousin's marital scheme aroused in Elizabeth no little degree of dissonance.

It is imperative that at least one of us marry and marry well, at that.

"And you, dear Lizzy, by your own accord seek a handsome man as the ideal husband, and save Mr. Darcy, of course, Mr. Wickham is by far the most handsome man we know."

"Phoebe, pray do not ascribe such a superficial attribute to me."

"Why, I am only repeating your own words."

"Words mentioned in jest, if I recall correctly."

Phoebe shrugged. "Nevertheless—"

So much as she did not wish to be an active party to her cousin's scheme of marital felicity for the twelve months, later, when Elizabeth was alone and at liberty to reflect on the events of the day, she could not help but think about her new acquaintance, Mr. Wickham.

The disdainful manner in which Mr. Darcy had regarded Mr. Wickham had been impossible not to discern.

No doubt, the two of them are acquaintances from the past. Even someone as haughty as Mr. Darcy would not show such a degree of disdain toward a complete stranger.

Elizabeth at once felt a bit ill at ease having thought of Mr. Darcy in such unflattering terms.

The morning he came to her aid after her muddy mishap while on her way to Netherfield Park, he had been the perfect gentleman—offering her kindness when he might easily have derided her.

Of course, he had quickly reverted to the gentleman she recalled meeting at the assembly when he was once again in the company of his friends—the pernicious Bingley sisters. Such varying emotions suffered on account of one particular man puzzled Elizabeth exceedingly.

Mr. Bingley, she felt she understood perfectly well. In essentials, the difference between Mr. Darcy and Mr. Bingley were akin to the differences between autumn and spring.

If there is indeed a history between the two gentlemen as I strongly suspect, perhaps in getting better acquainted with Mr. Wickham, I might be in a more advantageous position to sketch Mr. Darcy's character.

CHAPTER 11

THEIR MUTUAL ACQUAINTANCE

LONDON, ENGLAND - MAYFAIR

Upon entering the sitting room with a book in hand, Mrs. Annesley espied Georgiana sitting in the window seat, reading a missive. She cleared her throat in order to get the young lady's attention.

"Is that a letter from your brother?" the elderly woman asked.

Georgiana nodded. "Indeed. It is the second letter from him in as many weeks."

An elegant, mild-mannered woman who had known her share of beauty, Mrs. Annesley said, "Mr. Darcy is the most attentive—the best of brothers. What a kind and careful guardian he is." Her countenance beamed with gratitude. "Such brotherly affection is a blessing."

Georgiana could not agree more. To her way of thinking, her brother was the best man in the world, followed by her cousin Colonel Fitzwilliam, her co-guardian who shared the responsibility with her brother per her late father's direction.

Second to the colonel was her brother's friend Mr. Charles Bingley. Although Georgiana was given to consider that her esteem for Mr. Bingley would increase tremendously should she one day call herself his wife.

Though she was not at liberty to write to Mr. Bingley directly, she could, and she did take the opportunity to ask about the amiable young man whenever she wrote to her brother.

Her brother always responded in a manner that had taught Georgiana to hope that he was much in favor of an alliance between his friend and herself as evidenced by his inclusion that Mr. Bingley sends his fondest wishes in each correspondence.

What a striking contrast there was between her brother's response to a possible alliance between Mr. Bingley and her and his vitriolic response to a possible alliance between another gentleman of their mutual acquaintance and her: a Mr. George Wickham.

Each passing month taught her to appreciate her brother's stance. The other gentleman was not only too old for her what with him being so close to the wrong side of thirty, but he was also an opportunist. She discovered painfully that he was only interested in her for her fortune of thirty thousand pounds. The opportunity to spite her brother was a strong inducement as well.

Her brother had arrived in Ramsgate just in time to save her from what would have proved to be the biggest mistake of her life, an intractable decision that would have subjected her to misery of the acutest kind, to say nothing of the shame such a scandalous scheme would have heaped upon her noble family. However, despite the pain of the aborted event, there was a silver lining that came to light in the wake of it all, for it was shortly thereafter that her brother, in attempting to comfort her and convince her that her future for marital felicity was bright, gave the strongest hint of his hopes for an alliance between his close friend Charles Bingley and herself.

Charles Bingley was indeed everything a

gentleman ought to be. He was young and handsome and amiable, and he recommended himself very favorably to everyone whom he met. If he had any flaws at all, it had to do with his manner of becoming a part of her society. He was a very wealthy man to be sure, which really meant something to her, for in having his own fortune, her fortune could mean little to him; however, his fortune had been acquired in trade. He did not even have his own estate which meant he was not a landed gentleman, and as a result, he was beneath her in consequence.

Georgiana was convinced that was the reason her brother had so willingly gone with Mr. Bingley to Hertfordshire to help with the management of the latter's newly let estate, Netherfield Park. Under her brother's tutelage, Mr. Bingley would surely one day be the type of man her aristocratic family could be proud of.

By being in Hertfordshire with Mr. Bingley, my brother is really acting on behalf of my own best interest. Smiling, she held the letter to her chest. *To think I might one day be mistress of Mr. Bingley's home. I can hardly wait. He and I will be perfect for each other.*

Smiling, Georgiana folded her missive with the utmost care. She strode across the room to her writing desk, for as delighted as she was to have received a letter from her brother, Georgiana was just as happy to write to him in return. Even though Fitzwilliam was more than ten years her senior and often as much of a father to her since their father's untimely passing, he was her only sibling.

Upon retrieving her pen and inspecting it, she realized she could not go another day without mending it. She set about doing just that.

Steady to her purpose of performing a task she almost felt she could complete in her sleep; Georgiana's mind was more agreeably engaged in contemplation of what she would write to Fitzwilliam.

I suppose I ought to inquire about Netherfield's newest guests: the two sisters from the neighboring estate, especially the younger of the two, Miss Elizabeth.

Unable to recall the young lady's full name, Georgiana bit her lower lip. The next moment, her eyes widened. *Bennet! Miss Elizabeth Bennet.*

My brother made a concerted effort to include her in his missive. Why, he wrote two paragraphs, at least. He has never done anything like that before. It would be uncharitable not to acknowledge her.

Miss Elizabeth Bennet must really be an extraordinary

young woman to have garnered my brother's notice. Extraordinary, indeed.

When at last the task of mending her pen was concluded, Georgiana retrieved several sheets of paper from her desk with the intention of beginning a rather lengthy letter-writing campaign.

Surely if this young woman has managed to form such a favorable impression on my brother as his letters suggest, she is someone whom I should like to have the pleasure of meeting. I think I shall tell Fitzwilliam as much.

CHAPTER 12

HIS OWN PREFERENCE

During the ensuing days and weeks, Elizabeth meant to avail herself of every possible chance to learn all there was to know about not only Mr. Darcy but Mr. Wickham himself. Though she would never admit it to her cousin Phoebe, Elizabeth was beginning to admire the latter of the two gentlemen from Derbyshire very much.

In so many ways, Mr. Wickham was precisely what Mr. Darcy was not. Mr. Wickham was charming and amiable, and his own preference for Elizabeth was plain enough for everyone to see.

Despite subtle hints from Mr. Darcy that he was not entirely opposed to her, his changeable moods were sufficient to discourage any real affection on Elizabeth's part, which suited her just fine.

On that particular day, Elizabeth and Mr. Wickham trailed along behind the younger Bennet daughters on the path from Meryton to Longbourn.

She dared not even mention what she chiefly wished to discuss out of concern she was perhaps taking too much interest in the affairs of Mr. Darcy, as well as in the gentleman himself. Her curiosity, however, was unexpectedly relieved when Mr. Wickham broached the subject himself. He inquired how far Netherfield was from Meryton and, after receiving her answer, asked in a hesitating manner how long Mr. Darcy had been staying there.

"About a month," said Elizabeth. Unwilling to let the subject drop, she added, "His own estate is said to be among the finest in Derbyshire, I understand."

"Yes," replied Mr. Wickham, "his estate there is a noble one. A clear ten thousand per annum. You could not have met with a person more capable of giving you certain information on that head than myself, for I have been connected with his family in a particular manner from my infancy."

Elizabeth could not help but look surprised upon hearing this new information, for despite knowing both gentlemen hailed from Derbyshire, she had no reason to suspect a familial connection.

"You may well be surprised, Miss Bennet, at such an assertion, after seeing, as you probably might have, the very cold manner of our meeting the other day. Are you much acquainted with Mr. Darcy?"

"A little," cried Elizabeth. "I have spent several days in the same house with him." After a pause, she said, "I am afraid there are more than a few people who have met him who think him very disagreeable."

Wickham nodded knowingly. "And what of your own opinion?"

"Let me just say that I have yet to understand his character well enough to form a true opinion."

Again, her companion nodded. "I have no right to give my opinion as to his being agreeable or otherwise. I am not qualified to form one. I have known him too long and too well to be a fair judge. It is impossible for me to be impartial."

It was now Elizabeth's turn to nod. "Well, as I said, he is not at all liked by many in Hertfordshire. So many are disgusted with his pride."

"I cannot pretend to be sorry," said Wickham, after a short interruption, "that he or that any man should not be estimated beyond their deserts; but with him, I believe it does not often happen. The world is blinded by his fortune and consequence, or frightened by his high and imposing manners and sees him only as he chooses to be seen."

"I should take him, even on my slight acquaintance, to be a man of a rather uneven temperament."

Wickham only shook his head. "I wonder," said he, at the next opportunity of speaking, "whether he is likely to be in this country much longer."

"I do not at all know," Elizabeth replied. "I heard nothing of his going away when I was at Netherfield. I hope your plans will not be affected by his being in the neighborhood."

"Oh, no!" Wickham asserted. "It is not for me to be driven away by Mr. Darcy. If he wishes to avoid seeing me, he must go. We are not on friendly terms, and it always gives me pain to meet him, but I have no reason for avoiding him but what I might proclaim before all the world, a sense of very great ill-usage and most painful regrets at his being what he is.

"His father, the late Mr. Darcy, was one of the best men that ever breathed, and the truest friend I ever had. I can never be in company with this Mr. Darcy without being grieved to the soul by a thousand tender recollections. His behavior to myself has been scandalous, but I verily believe I could forgive him anything and everything, rather than disgracing the memory of his father."

Elizabeth found her interest in the subject increase and listened with all her heart, but the delicacy of it prevented further inquiry.

Mr. Wickham, as it turned out, needed no such inducement, for in continuing his speech about the circumstances which brought him to Hertfordshire in general and his joining the militia, specifically, Mr. Darcy's hand in the travesty could not help but be revealed.

"I have been a disappointed man, and my spirits will not bear solitude. I must have employment and society. A military life is not what I was intended for, but circumstances have now made it eligible. The church ought to have been my profession. I was brought up for the church, and I should at this time have been in possession of a most valuable living, had it pleased the gentleman we were speaking of just now."

"Indeed!"

"Yes—the late Mr. Darcy bequeathed me the next presentation of the best living in his gift. He was my godfather and excessively attached to me. I cannot do justice to his kindness. He meant to provide for me amply and thought he had done it, but when the living fell, it was given elsewhere."

"Good heavens!" cried Elizabeth. "How could that be? How could his will be disregarded? Why did you not seek legal redress?"

"There was just such an informality in the terms of the bequest as to give me no hope from law. A man of honor could not have doubted the intention, but Mr. Darcy chose to doubt it—or to treat it as a merely conditional recommendation and to assert that I had forfeited all claim to it by extravagance, imprudence—in short anything or nothing. Certain it is that the living became vacant two years ago, exactly as I was of an age to hold it, and that it was given to another man; and no less certain is it that I cannot accuse myself of having really done anything to deserve to lose it. I have a warm, unguarded temper, and I may have spoken my opinion of him, and to him, too freely. I can recall nothing worse. But the fact is we are very different sort of men and that he hates me."

"This is quite shocking! He deserves to be publicly disgraced," cried Elizabeth.

"Some time or other he will be—but it shall not be by me. Till I can forget his father, I can never defy or expose him."

Elizabeth honored him for such feelings and thought him more handsome than ever as he expressed them.

"But what," said she, after a pause, "can have been his motive? What can have induced him to behave so cruelly?"

"A thorough, determined dislike of me—a dislike which I cannot but attribute in some measure to jealousy. Had the late Mr. Darcy liked me less, his son might have borne with me better; but his father's uncommon attachment to me irritated him, I believe, very early in life. He had not a temper to bear the sort of competition in which we stood—the sort of preference which was often given me."

"I had not thought Mr. Darcy so bad as this," cried Elizabeth. "I had supposed him to be despising those whom he perceives as beneath him in consequence, but I did not suspect him of descending to such malicious revenge, such injustice, such inhumanity as this."

"Toward those whom he perceives as his inferiors, indeed," said Wickham as though reading Elizabeth's mind. "However, Mr. Darcy can please where he chooses. He does not want abilities. He can be an amiable companion if he thinks it worth his while. Among those who are at all his equals in consequence, he is a very different man from what he is to the less prosperous. His pride never deserts him; but with the rich, he is liberal-minded, just, sincere, rational, honorable, and perhaps agreeable—allowing something for fortune and figure."

Hearing this, Elizabeth immediately thought of the Bingleys. First, Mr. Bingley. *He is a sweet-tempered, amiable, charming man. He cannot know what Mr. Darcy really is.*

Next, she thought of Miss Caroline Bingley. *She is just the sort of female whom Mr. Darcy deserves.*

CHAPTER 13

OF A LONG DURATION

*P*hoebe was nothing if not persistent. Thus far, all of her efforts to garner Mr. Fitzwilliam Darcy's attention had been entirely in vain. She was not too nonsensical to discern the gentleman behaved toward her as though he barely even knew she was alive. This after having been in company with him on any number occasions since his arrival in Hertfordshire. It was as though he had completely mistaken her meaning when they were together in the Netherfield library, for she was certain her intentions were clear.

Tonight will be different, she silently declared, having prepared with more than the usual care for the long anticipated Netherfield ball.

"Have you seen Mr. Darcy?" Phoebe asked her cousin Elizabeth soon after she entered the ballroom.

Elizabeth shrugged. "I have not been looking for him."

"But you are looking for someone, no doubt," said the other young lady, her brow arched.

"Why would you say that?"

"Because of the manner in which you have been gazing about the room looking, here and there and everywhere in between." Pausing, she inspected her cousin from head to toe.

"You do look quite lovely this evening, no doubt in hopes of conquering all that remains unsubdued of your lover's heart. I shall spare you the trouble of passing the entire evening in such a lovelorn way. Your Mr. Wickham is not here. He is gone to London."

"How do you know that?" Elizabeth asked, her expression a little less cheerful than it had been before Phoebe's revelation.

"His friend, Mr. Denny, told my papa as we arrived together. I can tell by your dour expression my news meets with your disappointment, but you need not to be too terribly vexed for there are a great many handsome dancing partners gathered about from whom to choose."

Phoebe giggled. "I might even be prevailed upon to spare a set with *my* Mr. Darcy."

My Mr. Darcy, indeed, Elizabeth silently mocked her cousin's silly appellation for the gentleman. *I should be surprised if he dances with anyone at all save the pernicious Bingley sisters. Heaven forbid he might stand opposite young ladies whom he perceives beneath him in consequence.*

Supposing he was the cause of Mr. Wickham's absence, her ire she scarcely suppressed. *Had he not taken enough from Mr. Wickham? Did he mean to deny him the pleasure of a ball too?*

At that moment, the object of Phoebe's fascination entered the room. What a striking contrast he was to all the other gentlemen with his tall, handsome person and noble mien. His impeccable attire only added to his appeal.

Not that Elizabeth was affected, she promptly reminded herself.

"Oh! Cousin Lizzy," Phoebe cried. "I have a very good feeling about tonight. Pray, wish me good luck."

She was about to escape her cousin's side when Elizabeth took her by the arm. "Phoebe, where are you going?"

"Why, to speak with Mr. Darcy, of course. It has been far too long since I saw him last."

"But you cannot merely walk up to a man of his consequence and embark upon a conversation as though you were acquaintances of a long duration. He will think of it as an impertinence."

"For heaven's sakes, Lizzy. If I did not know better, I would say you were jealous."

"I most certainly am not!"

"Then, pray, stop behaving as though you are." Saying that, Phoebe jerked her arm away from her cousin's grip and stole away, intent on putting herself directly in Mr. Darcy's path.

Whether Mr. Darcy had deliberately thwarted young Phoebe's scheme, Elizabeth could not rightfully say. Perhaps it was merely a coincidence that no sooner than Phoebe was close enough to the gentleman to commence a conversation, he turned and walked away.

Elizabeth breathed a sigh in relief, for at least her cousin was too sensible to trail along behind him, and for that Elizabeth was grateful. She rather pitied Phoebe, owing to her cousin's foolish pursuit of the gentleman.

Later that evening, Phoebe got her second chance.

"Pray, do not look too eager ladies, but Mr. Darcy is coming our way," Phoebe said.

Upon approaching Charlotte, Elizabeth, and Phoebe, the gentleman bowed. The ladies curtsied. Despite what appeared to be her best effort to appear calm and collected, Phoebe's enthusiasm was evident. Not that Mr. Darcy would have noticed. It seemed he only had eyes for Elizabeth.

"Miss Elizabeth," he began, "may I have the next set?"

Elizabeth threw a quick glance at her cousin, who had nearly gasped out loud in the wake of her favorite's slight. What was Elizabeth to do? Break her poor cousin's heart? Or forgo her own felicity for the rest of the evening. Not that she was very happy about the gentleman damaging her cousin, even if unintentionally done.

Elizabeth swallowed. "Yes, you may, sir," she heard herself say.

With that, Mr. Darcy bowed again and then turned and walked away.

"Lizzy! How could you?" Phoebe cried. "I am

sure I shall never forgive you for such a blatant betrayal."

Before Elizabeth could fashion a response in her own defense, Phoebe hurried off. Elizabeth meant to follow her cousin, but Charlotte seized hold of her hand.

"Let her go," Charlotte beseeched.

"Oh, Charlotte! What have I done?"

"You did the only thing you could do, given the situation. Had you refused Mr. Darcy you would have been obliged to eschew dancing for the rest of the evening. Trust me, Phoebe will realize you had no other choice in the matter soon enough."

"It is not only Phoebe's wounded pride that concerns me but rather my own sentiments toward the gentleman that trouble me as well. How am I to endure standing opposite Mr. Darcy after what he has done?"

"What has he done?" Charlotte begged.

"Charlotte, you know very well how much Mr. Darcy and Mr. Wickham dislike each other. I have learned over the course of the evening that Mr. Darcy is the reason Mr. Wickham is not in attendance this evening."

"What can any grievances between the two of

them have to do with you?"

"How can you even ask me such a question? Who that knows of Mr. Wickham's misfortunes as a consequence of Mr. Darcy's ill-treatment would not side with the former? Men of Mr. Darcy's ilk are far too eager to wield their power at the expense of the less fortunate."

"Eliza, you must allow that there are two sides to every story and thus far, you have only been privy to the so-called injured party's account."

"If Mr. Darcy is innocent of Mr. Wickham's charges, then let him come forth and defend himself. Unless and until he does, I shall stand by the more amiable of the two."

"I caution you, dearest Eliza, do not be a simpleton and allow your fancy for Mr. Wickham to make you appear unpleasant in the eyes of a man ten times his consequence. Besides, has Mr. Darcy not always been a consummate gentleman toward you?"

Shortly after Charlotte's speech, Elizabeth stood alone on the balcony. She needed a breath of fresh air as she pondered her intimate friend's words, as well as prepared herself to spend the next half hour dancing with Mr. Darcy.

Despite every attempt to forget the day he

encountered her on the lane on her way to Netherfield and how comforted she felt by his attentiveness toward her, her body's reaction to his nearness was always somewhat unsettling.

Charlotte is correct, Elizabeth silently confessed. *There are two sides to every story. But how am I to discern any measure of truth from Mr. Darcy? He is so taciturn and aloof. I doubt he and I will exchange more than a few quick words if any at all.*

Shall I comment on the size of the room and the number of couples? Would that draw him out? Perhaps I might mention that I find private balls more pleasurable than public balls. No doubt that is something the two of us might have in common. If I recall correctly, he seemed most uncomfortable at the Meryton assembly.

As was often the case whenever Elizabeth allowed herself to dwell too long on the enigma that was Mr. Darcy, the memory of his nearness as he led her undetected to Jane's apartment intruded.

He had been so kind and courteous—exactly how a gentleman ought to be in view of my circumstances. She smiled a little. She wrapped her arms about her shoulders in remembrance of how comforting she had found his great coat draping her—how protected she had felt.

Never had she felt that way in any gentleman's company. Not even Mr. Wickham's.

I wonder if I shall ever feel that way again?

Elizabeth shook her head. *I must not allow myself to think this way.* Her spirits rising just a bit, she smiled. *Besides, what would my cousin Phoebe think?*

Later that evening, Elizabeth, once again, found herself all alone on the balcony. What a disaster the past half hour had been. Why had Mr. Darcy asked her to dance if he only meant to bait her into an argument about Mr. Wickham? Elizabeth searched her memory for the impertinent question on his part that had set their heated intercourse in motion: *"Do you and your sisters often walk to Meryton?"*

His eyes thoroughly belied the innocence of his question. He had seen her conversing with Mr. Wickham. He was chastising her. By what right did he have to judge her for appreciating the character of a man whose character was in such stark contrast to his own?

She had answered in the affirmative, and, unable to resist the temptation, added, "When you met us there the other day, we had just been forming a new acquaintance."

The effect was immediate. A deeper shade of

hauteur overspread his features, but he said not a word, and Elizabeth, though blaming herself for her own weakness, could not go on. At length, Darcy said in a constrained manner, "Mr. Wickham is blessed with such happy manners as may ensure his making friends—whether he may be equally capable of retaining them, is less certain."

"He has been so unlucky as to lose your friendship," Elizabeth had replied with emphasis, "and in a manner which he is likely to suffer from all his life."

A timely interruption by Sir William Lucas served to diffuse the increasing ire between them; however, the resulting reprieve did not last long.

His surprising attempt at pleasant, albeit threadbare talk of books, had resulted in yet another contentious discussion of Elizabeth's attempt to sketch his character.

"And what is your success?" Mr. Darcy had inquired.

"I do not get on at all," Elizabeth had replied, shaking her head. "I hear such different accounts of you as puzzle me exceedingly."

"I can readily believe," he answered gravely, "that reports may vary greatly with respect to me;

and I could wish, Miss Bennet, that you were not to sketch my character at the present moment, as there is reason to fear that the performance would reflect no credit on either."

"But if I do not take your likeness now, I may never have another opportunity."

"I would by no means suspend any pleasure of yours," he had coldly replied.

Gazing at the moon high above, Elizabeth pursed her lips. *"I would by no means suspend any pleasure of yours."*

What did Mr. Darcy mean in speaking to me in such a fashion?

Tidying her hair just a bit in preparation to rejoin the ballroom gaieties, Elizabeth released a frustrated sigh.

Why am I even thinking about any of this? Mr. Darcy's reason for asking me to dance more than likely was meant to frustrate Miss Bingley. Those two are so much alike, I begin to wonder why he does not marry her and in so doing answer her prayers.

Not too displeased by this conjecture, Elizabeth pursed her lips. *Of course, my cousin Phoebe would be terribly upset, but I, for one, would rejoice in his reaping such a prize as Miss Caroline Bingley as his bride after everything he has done to poor Mr. Wickham.*

CHAPTER 14

AN EQUAL SHARE OF BENEFIT

From complete embarrassment as a consequence of her family's unseemly behavior at the ball, to the mortification she suffered in her own home an hour or so earlier, Elizabeth was certain she did not deserve even a smidgen of the anguish she had endured.

Her younger sisters, Kitty and Lydia, had made themselves entirely ridiculous with their girlish antics in pursuit of the officers in attendance. Her sister Mary had garnered the censure of all the other young ladies in the room with her lackluster exhibition on the pianoforte. Her own father had rendered poor Mary's humiliation complete by interrupting her performance with what should have been a gentle admonishment but in effect had rendered his daughter heartbroken.

Then there was the unseemly behavior of Mr. Collins, which further cast a disparaging pall on Elizabeth's family, for upon learning of the connection between his noble patroness Lady Catherine de Bourgh and Mr. Darcy, her cousin embarked upon a most sycophantic attack of the latter.

By then, Elizabeth was certain the evening could not get any worse. But alas, it did. Mrs. Bennet, who never really liked Mr. Darcy from the start, owing to his haughty nature and ill-mannered treatment of her neighbors, seemed to delight in the idea of boasting aloud that her daughter Jane and the handsome and amiable Mr. Bingley were soon to be married.

While this was undoubtedly the favorite wish of Elizabeth, she was not so nonsensical as to voice her opinion out loud in such a setting and within hearing distance of someone who for reasons of his own might not relish such a prospect.

She could not help frequently glancing at Mr. Darcy throughout her mother's uncouth discourse, and every glance convinced her of what she dreaded, for although he was not always looking at her mother, she was convinced that his attention was invariably fixed by her. The expression of his face changed gradually from indignant contempt to a composed and steady gravity.

The only comfort Elizabeth had subsequent to the exchange was her belief in Mr. Bingley's love for her dearest sister, Jane. Surely a man who was so much in love with Jane as Mr. Bingley was would never allow the deficiencies in her family to discourage his affections.

The deep sigh of relief that Elizabeth exhaled was rendered mute by the gasp of abhorrence that escaped her some hours later.

"Believe me, my dear Miss Elizabeth, that your modesty, so far from doing you any disservice, rather adds to your other perfections. You would have been less amiable in my eyes had there not been this little unwillingness; but allow me to assure you that I have your respected mother's permission for this address. You can hardly doubt the purport of my discourse. However your natural delicacy may lead you to dissemble, my attentions have been too marked to be mistaken. Almost as soon as I entered the house, I singled you out as the companion of my future life."

Elizabeth could not believe it. She would not believe it. Her father had warned her that Mr. Collins had come to Longbourn with the purpose of choosing a wife.

What have I done to garner such an undesirable distinction other than ignore the man and pretend he does not exist? This little unwillingness indeed!

Even if she had felt anything other than utter revulsion for the ridiculous man, a proposal such as he then put forth would never suit. In response to Elizabeth's adamant refusal of his offer of marriage, Mr. Collins had further insulted her thusly:

"You should take it into further consideration that, in spite of your manifold attractions, it is by no means certain that another offer of marriage may ever be made you. Your portion is unhappily so small that it will in all likelihood undo the effects of your loveliness and amiable qualifications. As I must therefore conclude that you are not serious in your rejection of me, I shall choose to attribute it to your wish of increasing my love by suspense, according to the usual practice of elegant females."

All of her further protests fell on deaf ears, leaving Elizabeth but one alternative—that being to flee the man's presence. Even as she hastened toward the door, she heard him say, "When I do myself the honor of speaking to you next on the subject, I shall hope to receive a more favorable answer than you have now given me."

Having immediately after that sought and received her father's blessing on her decision to refuse her cousin's hand, Elizabeth found her sister Jane in the garden. By now the entire household was in an uproar over Elizabeth's behavior and thus little by way of an explanation of what all had been said and done was needed. And as Elizabeth was not designed for being discontented, she put forth a lighter view of her present dilemma.

"Pray, Phoebe does not soon hear of what I have done, for she will surely regard it as a sign that I am in love with *her* Mr. Darcy," Elizabeth said.

"Well, Lizzy, he did dance with you at the ball. I do not recall seeing him standing opposite Phoebe on the dance floor."

The discomfort she had felt in being an unintentional party to her cousin's slight caused Elizabeth's pulse to quicken. "Jane, what are you saying?" Elizabeth asked, hoping Jane did not see how those words had affected her.

"All I am saying is perhaps Phoebe does have cause for concern." She reached her hand out to her sister. "Not that you would deliberately set out to disappoint our cousin's hopes, but as for Mr. Darcy, I dare say he behaves as though he does not even know our cousin is alive."

Elizabeth shrugged. "I am afraid you are correct. However, I have to believe that her interest in the gentleman is largely a consequence of her little matrimonial scheme. If she really knew what Mr. Darcy is like, I suspect she might not be nearly so enamored of him."

"I confess that Mr. Darcy has not made the most favorable impression on our acquaintances, but those who know him best: Mr. Bingley, Miss Bingley, Mr. and Mrs. Hurst, all of them think very highly of him."

"And what of Mr. Wickham's opinion? Are his feelings to be completely disregarded?"

"I must confess that there is a history between the two of them which none of us completely comprehend—not even Mr. Bingley, but I am rather inclined to rely upon the good opinion of the many to the ill-opinion of the one."

"Dearest Jane, that is because you are too generous to think meanly of anyone. And while I have been accused of being far too apt to willfully misunderstand, in such a case as this, I believe I understand both Mr. Darcy and Mr. Wickham well enough to know which of the two to side with."

"I say you ought to keep an open mind and give both gentlemen an equal share of benefit as well as doubt."

Elizabeth said, "And I say this conversation is much too consequential after the morning I have suffered. I would much rather talk about you and your Mr. Bingley. I do not mind confessing that I spent a fair amount of time admiring the two of you at the ball. I think he loves you very much. As much as I do not wish to sound like Mama, especially after the horrendous spectacle she made of herself in front of Mr. Darcy at supper, I do believe she may be on to something."

"What did Mama do?"

"Oh! Other than alienate the gentleman, perhaps forever, she did nothing for you to worry about. So long as Mr. Bingley is in love with you, that is to say. And I am convinced he is."

"Dearest, Lizzy, I pray what you are saying is true. I am beginning to depend on it."

"Mrs. Jane Bingley née Bennet. This must certainly meet with Phoebe's approval. One of the four of us is soon to be married with at least ten months for the rest of us to follow suit."

"Lizzy, if I have said it once, I have said it a hundred times… you are incorrigible."

CHAPTER 15

SUFFICIENT ENCOURAGEMENT

*T*wo days had passed, and yet Elizabeth had neither seen nor heard from her cousin Phoebe. In Elizabeth's busy mind that could mean but one thing.

Cousin Phoebe is still very vexed because of what happened at the Netherfield ball.

This odd behavior on her cousin's part was causing Elizabeth to suspect that Phoebe really did fancy Mr. Darcy after all.

What a shame if such were indeed the case, Elizabeth thought to herself, having since learned from Mr. Wickham that Mr. Darcy was intended for his cousin, a Miss Anne de Bourgh: the only child of the gentleman's noble aunt, Lady Catherine de Bourgh.

She shrugged. Even if he were not engaged, Elizabeth doubted Phoebe stood a chance of garnering Mr. Darcy's favor. Not that she dared confess her opinion on the matter to her cousin, for she knew her relation well enough to know there would have been no point.

If Mr. Darcy's behavior has not been enough to teach Phoebe of her own insignificance in his eyes, certainly nothing I might do or say will convince her. Phoebe is young and fanciful, and as an only child, she is spoiled and used to having her way. I truly believe she will finally see the truth for herself once she believes it and not a moment before.

A disquiet soon took over the halls of Longbourn and sent Jane racing past Elizabeth, ignoring all entreaties to explain what had unfolded, up the stairs, and into her room.

Elizabeth immediately set off behind her sister. Pushing the door open, Elizabeth espied Jane sitting by the window, staring blankly outside, and clutching a letter in her hand.

Jane, having no desire to keep her dearest sister in further suspense, handed the letter over. "It is from Caroline Bingley, written in part on behalf of her brother."

Elizabeth accepted it at once. Before she could

open it, Jane said, "What it contains has surprised me a good deal, for by now the entire party has left Netherfield and with no intention of coming back again."

In heightened dismay, Elizabeth began reading the letter in silence, not wishing to subject her sister to any further pain in having to hear the words aloud:

"When my brother left us, he imagined that the business which took him to London might be concluded in three or four days. But as we are certain it cannot be so, and at the same time convinced that when Charles gets to town, he will be in no hurry to leave it again, we have determined on following him thither, that he may not be obliged to spend his vacant hours in a comfortless hotel. Many of my acquaintances are already there for the winter; I wish that I could hear that you, my dearest friend, had any intention of making one of the crowd—but of that, I despair. I sincerely hope your Christmas in Hertfordshire may abound in the gaieties which that season generally brings, and that your beaux will be so numerous as to prevent your feeling the loss of those of whom we shall deprive you."

Here, Elizabeth scoffed. She never did care for Miss Bingley, and now she cared for the lady even less.

Jane said, "You may as well read what she says aloud."

"Are you certain, Jane?"

Jane nodded, encouraging Elizabeth to read aloud:

"Mr. Darcy is impatient to see his sister; and, to confess the truth, we are scarcely less eager to meet her again. I really do not think Georgiana Darcy has her equal for beauty, elegance, and accomplishments; and the affection she inspires in Louisa and myself is heightened into something still more interesting, from the hope we dare entertain of her being hereafter our sister. I do not know whether I ever before mentioned to you my feelings on this subject, but I will not leave the country without confiding them, and I trust you will not esteem them unreasonable."

Here, Elizabeth paused. "Jane, surely you do not believe a word of this."

Jane merely shrugged, which was sufficient encouragement for Elizabeth to read on.

"My brother admires her greatly already; he will have frequent opportunity now of seeing her on the most intimate footing; her relations all wish the connection as much as his own, and a sister's partiality is not misleading me, I think, when I call

Charles most capable of engaging any woman's heart. With all these circumstances to favor an attachment, and nothing to prevent it, am I wrong, my dearest Jane, in indulging the hope of an event which will secure the happiness of so many?"

Mrs. Bennet's appalling behavior immediately sprang to mind. *Could Mr. Darcy be complicit in any of this? Was he just as anxious to separate Mr. Bingley and Jane as was Caroline Bingley?*

A part of her desperately hoped such was not the case. That part of her that had decided to allow him the benefit of the doubt.

Convinced mainly that this was Caroline's doing and Caroline's alone, Elizabeth folded the letter and said, "I believe you ought to go to town as well. I am certain our uncle and aunt Gardiner will be delighted to have you. Once you are there, you must do all in your power to let Mr. Bingley know you are in London. Only then will you be in the position to expose his sister's lies and half-truths for what they are."

Jane shook her head. "I should never willingly pursue the affections of a gentleman who does not truly care for me. What would be the point?"

"Bingley does care for you. You know he does,

and his sister knows it too, which is precisely the reason she means to separate you two. Come, we shall speak with Papa and Mama about your going to London. They will no doubt encourage the scheme, and then we shall write the necessary letters."

Later that same day, Elizabeth's friend Charlotte sought out a private conference wishing to share happy news of her own. By Elizabeth's expression, however, the intelligence was met with anything but pleasure.

Elizabeth colored. She stared, and when she finally found her voice in the wake of her friend's profession, she cried, "Can this day get any worse?"

Taken aback, Charlotte said, "That is not very charitable of you. I knew you would be surprised by what I have come to say—perhaps even a little disappointed, but I did not expect you to be uncivil."

"Oh, Charlotte, pray you will forgive me. I did not mean to give offense—truly, I did not. Of course, I am surprised, but I know you are acting according to your own best interest. I will not judge you too severely as a result." Elizabeth wrapped her arms about her shoulders.

"When I complained about today getting worse, I was referring to the Netherfield party's precipitous exodus to London and more specifically a letter that Miss Bingley wrote to Jane, purportedly on Mr. Bingley's behalf, which stated his intention not to return to this part of the country in the foreseeable future.

"Oh, Charlotte! You can surely comprehend the depths of poor Jane's heartbreak."

"Oh, my!" Charlotte cried, nodding in agreement.

"Jane's heartbreak aside," Elizabeth continued, "My mama is nearly inconsolable to have lost not one but two prospective sons-in-law in under a week. She blames Jane for not doing enough to make Mr. Bingley fall in love with her, but not nearly so much as she blames me for—well surely you know what transpired between Mr. Collins and me."

She reached out her hand to her friend. "Again, I do not bear any ill will toward you for accepting him, but the news of your engagement will surely drive Mama to distraction."

"Undoubtedly," Charlotte said. "And if I have any regrets at all about how my own future felicity came to be, the implications for your mother's peace of mine are at the center of it all."

Charlotte did not stay much longer, and Elizabeth was then left to reflect on what she had heard. It was a long time before she became at all reconciled to the idea of so unsuitable a match. The strangeness of Mr. Collins's making two offers of marriage within three days was nothing in comparison of his being now accepted.

She had always felt that Charlotte's opinion of matrimony was not exactly like her own, but she had not supposed it to be possible that, when called into action, she would have sacrificed every better feeling to worldly advantage. Charlotte as the wife of Mr. Collins was a most humiliating picture! And to the pang of a friend disgracing herself and sunk in her esteem, was added the distressing conviction that it was impossible for that friend to be tolerably happy in the lot she had chosen.

The predicament Elizabeth now found herself in did not sit well with her temperament at all, and thus she chose to consider things in a more satisfying light.

For every disadvantage inherent in the events of the last day there must certainly be an advantage. This thought gave Elizabeth a bit of comfort, for if Phoebe was really more fascinated with her marital scheme than she was infatuated with Mr. Darcy, then any displeasure that would arise as a result of his abrupt leave-taking would surely be offset by the pleasure of Charlotte's pending nuptials.

CHAPTER 16

TRUTH BE TOLD

LONDON, ENGLAND - MAYFAIR

Miss Georgiana Darcy, a young girl of sixteen, found it ironic indeed that she had her own establishment and yet the young woman who might one day be her sister, if the two ladies had their way, was much older than she, but enjoyed no such arrangement.

I suppose I must credit my good fortune in that regard to the vast disparity in our respective brothers' wealth.

After handing her guest a freshly poured cup of tea, Georgiana said, "Dearest Miss Bingley, pray tell me how does your brother, Mr. Bingley, get along?"

"Oh, Miss Darcy, as our mutual goal is one day to enjoy the privilege of calling ourselves sisters, is it not time we cease with the formalities and address each other by our given names? Please call me Caroline."

Being of the same mind as her friend, the younger woman smiled. "Very well, and according to the usual way of doing these things, pray call me Georgiana."

"Delightful." Miss Bingley took a sip from her dainty cup. At length, she said, "You know I do not wish to speak out of turn, but have you given any consideration at all to my suggestion that you speak with your brother, Mr. Darcy, about your giving up this establishment and residing with him here in town. My brother Charles is frequently at Darcy House, and you two would always be crossing each other's path."

Georgiana knew that her guest had a secondary, if not primary, motive for her advice, for Miss Bingley called on her nearly every day—her eyes always searching, and her ears always perched for some sign of Fitzwilliam's presence. She knew better than anyone that Miss Bingley was far more interested in becoming her future sister by way of an alliance between her brother,

Fitzwilliam Darcy, and herself than she was interested in such an alliance between Georgiana and Mr. Bingley.

Truth be told, Georgiana was not sure how much she liked the idea of an alliance between her brother and Miss Bingley.

There is something about Miss Bingley—rather Caroline, that simply does not ring true, and I am starting to suspect she would not make my brother very happy. She arched her brow in silent contemplation.

A part of me suspects she is more interested in being the next mistress of Pemberley more so than anything else.

Not that it mattered to Georgiana. Her brother had not remained a single man for seven and twenty years by accident.

I know that he is extraordinarily fastidious and will not be easily persuaded by the likes of a mercenary female. I shall have no reason to concern myself in that regard.

Georgiana's real opinion of Miss Bingley as the next mistress of Pemberley aside, she knew in her heart that she would one day refer to the other young woman as a sister. Indeed, she also knew she owed Miss Bingley a great debt for having prevented Charles Bingley from making a grave mistake while they were all in Hertfordshire last autumn.

Charles Bingley, being the charming gentleman that he was, had apparently given one of the local young ladies the impression that he was in love with her. Had it not been for her brother, Fitzwilliam Darcy, and Miss Bingley, Mr. Bingley might well have found himself ensnared in a most disadvantageous alliance with the young woman who, according to Miss Bingley's accounting, was on the verge of spinsterhood, owing to the cunning of the young lady's eager and dreadfully uncouth mother.

Poor Charles. To be so willfully misunderstood when he was only being his charming, gregarious self. Why, I am told the two were rarely even in company with each other and never alone, and yet the mother had boasted aloud of an imminent wedding at Netherfield Park. What nerve!

"I have not approached my brother just yet," said Georgiana. "I believe timing is everything. Besides, his annual trip to Kent to visit our aunt Lady Catherine de Bourgh and our cousin Anne is approaching soon."

Miss Bingley's teacup clinked against the saucer. "How tiring it must be for poor Mr. Darcy to always be expected to spend part of the London Season amid such tiring company," Miss Bingley opined.

Georgiana arched her brow. "Pray, have a care, Caroline. The tiring company you are referring to are my family. They mean a great deal to me as well as my brother. Besides, I do not believe my brother is the least bit disappointed in visiting every year, else he certainly would not do so. He is his own master, after all."

"But, of course, you are correct," replied the other young lady knowingly. "I suppose I shall one day find myself obliged to spend part of the Season in Kent as well."

"Until such time, my brother relies upon our cousin Colonel Fitzwilliam's companionship on his annual visits."

"Oh, but surely when he has chosen a wife, who shall better afford a more lasting convenience in said regard, all of that will change. Speaking of which, I do hope your aunt has given up the hope of an alliance between Mr. Darcy and your cousin Anne."

Georgiana could not help but recall Lady Catherine's favorite refrain regarding that particular matter: *"The engagement between them is of a peculiar kind. From their infancy, they have been intended for each other. It was the favorite wish of his mother, as well as of her own. While in their cradles, we planned the union."*

Shaking her head, she silently scoffed. "My aunt is very determined—that is one fact I dare not deny. But I am sure I would not worry about any of that if I were you."

Smiling, Miss Bingley placed her cup on the saucer and set both aside on a nearby table. Reaching out to the younger woman, she seized her hand and gave it a gentle squeeze. "Dearest Georgiana, I simply cannot tell you how much hearing you say that means to me. I declare you are the kindest person I know. My brother could not wish for a more advantageous alliance than an alliance with you, and I shall do everything in my power to see that it comes about. Between your brother and me, your happiness with my brother is assured."

CHAPTER 17

BEYOND EXPRESSION

HUNSFORD - SPRING 1812

The ensuing weeks and months had done little to calm Mrs. Bennet's vexations as well as her complaints of being ill-used, not only by her own daughters but by her husband and Mr. Bingley too. Added to her lengthy list of lamentations was the fact the militia had decamped from the environs, taking away any chance that one of her daughters might garner the affections of one of the officers.

Jane had also journeyed to town to stay with her uncle and aunt, Mr. and Mrs. Gardiner, from Cheapside. As reluctant as Jane had been to employ such measures, Elizabeth had to believe that the prospect of crossing paths with Mr. Bingley was a strong inducement. She needed no more evidence than this to persuade herself that Jane really did love Mr. Bingley with all her heart, and anyone who might attempt to discredit her sister's feelings would surely meet with Elizabeth's extreme displeasure.

With so little in Hertfordshire to divert her, Elizabeth was overjoyed to receive a letter from her now married friend Charlotte inviting her to come to Hunsford for a visit. As Phoebe had long since set aside her assumed grievances against Elizabeth, she gave the strongest hints of wanting to travel to that part of the country as well. And thither the two young ladies journeyed.

Little did Elizabeth know or even have reason to suspect that a few weeks after their arrival, she would be the recipient of yet another unwelcome proposal of marriage. As fate would have it, not very far away in Rosings Park, the home of her cousin Mr. Collins's noble patroness, Lady Catherine de Bourgh, stayed Mr. Fitzwilliam Darcy himself as well as another, a rather amiable gentleman: Colonel Fitzwilliam. Both were her ladyship's nephews and most honored guests.

There Elizabeth sat in her friend's parlor listening to the former - the proud Mr. Darcy - professing his ardent love for her.

To add insult to injury, he told her his profession was being made against his better judgment even against his will.

"In vain I have struggled. It will not do. My feelings will not be repressed. You must allow me to tell you how ardently I admire and love you."

Elizabeth's astonishment was beyond expression. She stared, colored, doubted, and was silent. Looming in the shadows of her mind throughout his ensuing speech was a conversation she had earlier that same day with Mr. Darcy's cousin Colonel Fitzwilliam.

Owing to Mr. Collins's devotion to his noble patroness, whose extensive property, Rosings Park, abutted his own humble abode, frequent engagements with her ladyship were unavoidable. Time spent in Mr. Wickham's company in the wake of the Netherfield party's leave-taking had afforded her ample opportunity to learn all she needed to know about the grand lady as well as her daughter. Thus she was wholly prepared for the rudeness, the condescension, and even the thinly veiled disdain from the haughty aristocrat upon meeting Lady Catherine.

Making the colonel's acquaintance rendered time spent in her ladyship's company and even Mr. Darcy's, to an extent, far more tolerable than Elizabeth might have suspected. Indeed, she liked the colonel very much.

An amiable gentleman who fell readily into conversation with everyone whom he met, the colonel had spoken rather candidly of Mr. Darcy's recent service to his young friend Charles Bingley by preventing him from entering a most disadvantageous alliance to a young woman.

When asked about the reason for Mr. Darcy's interference, the colonel had cited the young lady's family as the principal concern. That and what his cousin had perceived as unequal affections on the part of the young lady toward Bingley himself.

Elizabeth's ire in hearing this had not diminished one bit and any goodwill Mr. Darcy had managed to accrue during their time together in Kent when he had accidentally met her during her solitary rambles about the lanes was now deep in arrears.

Now the proud man stood before her speaking

of her inferiority and that of her family—how his own family would suffer as a result of such an unequal alliance. All these things and yet he was willing to look past them if she would but do him the honor of accepting his hand.

When, finally, it was Elizabeth's turn to speak, she addressed him in a manner akin to that which he had afforded her.

"Sir," she began, "in such cases as this, it is, I believe, the established mode to express a sense of obligation for the sentiments avowed, however unequally they may be returned. It is natural that obligation should be felt, and if I could feel gratitude, I would now thank you. But I cannot, and I shall not."

"Are you—are you rejecting me?" Mr. Darcy inquired in a manner which suggested he was not used to being denied anything.

"I am sorry to have occasioned pain of any sort to you. It has been most unconsciously done."

His complexion pale with anger and the disturbance of his mind visible in every feature, he needed to know why—what could possibly be her reason for rejecting his suit with so little thought and even less civility?

Her temper she dared not vouch for, especially in the wake of the colonel's confession and Mr. Darcy's own confirmation by way of his unflattering proposal. Drawing a deep breath, Elizabeth stood and approached him. "I might as well inquire why with so evident a desire of offending and insulting me, you chose to tell me that you liked me against your will, against your reason, and even against your character? Was not this some excuse for incivility if I was uncivil?"

She drew even closer while the gentleman remained in the same attitude. "But I have other provocations. You know I have. Had not my feelings for you been indifferent or had they even been favorable, do you think that any consideration would tempt me to accept the man who has been the means of ruining, perhaps forever, the happiness of a most beloved sister?"

As though completely unaffected by Elizabeth's speech, Mr. Darcy said nothing, which only served to provoke her ire even more.

"Your silence speaks volumes. Mr. Darcy!" Her voice pained, she asked. "How could you do it? How dare you separate two people in love, exposing one to the censure of the world for caprice and instability, and the other to its derision for disappointed hopes, and involving them both in misery of the acutest kind?"

"Why would I not do everything in my power to separate my friend from your sister? Why would I not rejoice in my success? I know my friend well enough to know such an unequal alliance would redound entirely to his detriment. Toward him, I have been kinder than toward myself."

"Then you must congratulate yourself—or rather thank me for sparing you a fate akin to that which you saved your friend."

"Perhaps it would be better if we cease speaking on this matter."

"I beg to differ, sir, for I have another grievance against you—one I dare not suppress any longer than I have already."

It was now Mr. Darcy's turn to close what little distance there was between them. "And what, pray tell, is that?"

"It is the matter of your ill-treatment of Mr. Wickham—one with whom you cannot deny having shared an amiable past and yet your actions toward him have proved to be deplorable."

"Wickham!" Mr. Darcy repeated, his voice

filled with disdain. "You take an eager interest in that gentleman's concerns."

"Who that knows what his misfortunes have been can help feeling an interest in him?"

"His misfortunes!" repeated Darcy contemptuously. "Yes, his misfortunes have been great indeed."

She dug her nails into her palms. "And of your infliction," cried Elizabeth with energy. "You have reduced him to his present state of poverty. You have withheld the advantages which you must know to have been designed for him. You have deprived the best years of his life of that independence which was no less his due than his desert. You have done all this! Yet, you can treat the mention of his misfortune with contempt and ridicule."

"And this," said Mr. Darcy, "is your opinion of me! This is the estimation in which you hold me! I thank you for explaining it so fully. My faults, according to this calculation, are heavy indeed!"

Unbeknown to either Mr. Darcy or Elizabeth, the two of them were not alone—not entirely, for

Phoebe had also escaped Rosings, where all of the Hunsford party save Elizabeth were having tea, soon after Mr. Darcy abruptly took his leave. There she had stood just outside the slightly ajar parlor door for the better part of the very unsuspecting couple's contentious intercourse.

Having heard more than enough, Phoebe had raced up the stairs to the room she shared with her cousin.

Breathless, she did not know what had alarmed her more: that the man whom she had fancied for so long had not proposed to her but to her cousin, or that her cousin had been foolish enough to refuse him.

A refusal that was not even borne out of Lizzy's loyalty to me, but out of her affection for Lieutenant Wickham.

Phoebe had arrived just in time to hear Mr. Darcy speak the words that cut her deeply.

"You must allow me to tell you how ardently I admire and love you."

The entirety of all she heard played out in her mind. The gentleman's words, though eloquently spoken, had been riddled with disparagement about her cousin and others whom she held dear, but what had he said that was untrue?

Truth be told, she had entertained the idea that Mr. Darcy's apparent reticence toward her was borne out of her family's circumstances, although unlike the Bennet girls, Phoebe had a dowry which must certainly negate such concerns.

As a consequence of being the eldest son, Mr. Phillips had also inherited the larger share of his father's meager fortune, a portion of which he had invested wisely and thus designated as his only daughter's dowry. She, in turn, had been taught by a governess, for her father's family had insisted upon it, and she had frequently gone to London for the benefit of the masters.

A young woman with a thorough knowledge of music, singing, drawing, dancing, and the modern languages, Phoebe also excelled in painting tables, covering screens, and netting purses.

Unlike her cousin's lackluster exhibition on the pianoforte at Rosings at Lady Catherine de Bourgh's behest, Phoebe's exhibition had been exemplary.

Any man—even one of Mr. Darcy's consequence, would be lucky to have her.

Returning her mind to the real culprit that evening, Phoebe recalled her cousin's rejection of

Mr. Darcy's hand: *"You are the last man in the world whom I could ever be prevailed on to marry."*

Phoebe shook her head. *Yes, there was Mr. Darcy's interference with Jane and Mr. Bingley, but I dare say that had Lizzy been of a mind to rectify that misfortune what better way than to accept the hand of the one person best positioned to reunite them?*

Her understanding of her cousin's motives grew clearer upon each recollection of what she had heard.

I am persuaded that Lizzy's love for Mr. Wickham is the primary motivation for what she has done.

The thought that her cousin had led Mr. Darcy on crossed her mind.

Lizzy was never truly in favor of an alliance between Mr. Darcy and me. I am persuaded she did everything in her power to draw him in. She did not want him, and she did not want me to have him either.

She nodded. *Now that I think about it, I believe I was too hasty in dismissing my earlier suspicions about my cousin when we were at the Netherfield ball and she used her feminine arts and allurements to turn Mr. Darcy's head. Perhaps, she employed her duplicitous stratagems to her advantage and thereby my disadvantage long before then—before I arrived at Netherfield during Jane's convalescence, and yet again once I took my leave. Who is to say to what lengths Lizzy might have gone to thwart my efforts to garner Mr. Darcy's affection for me?*

"Very well," Phoebe said out loud. "Turn about is fair play," she added, reciting a phrase often used by her cousins and herself during their younger days.

Even if a tiny part of her owned that her cousin was not entirely to blame for her favorite beau's defection, her bruised ego whispered, *I no longer wish to be in such close proximity to the person who has been the means of injuring me. Let Mr. Darcy pine away for Lizzy to his heart's content. I do not want anyone's seconds, even if he is so very rich.*

She drew a deep breath. "Mr. Darcy is nothing to me now, and I have Lizzy to thank for that. I will teach her not to cross me again."

Her desire to get away from Hunsford and thereby get away from her conniving cousin grew more urgent with each passing minute. Would she go to London to spend time with Jane? Would she return to Hertfordshire to the sanctuary of her own home—her own things?

Although Phoebe's father had settled in Hertfordshire some decades earlier, her father's family was from Brighton. What was more, Phoebe's aunt had prevailed on her many times to come to

Brighton for a visit. She arched her brow in contemplation as another one of her brilliant ideas took form.

Cousin Lizzy's precious Mr. Wickham has recently gone to Brighton with the militia. I believe the time has come for me to accept my aunt's invitation for a long overdue visit.

Prepare yourself to know just how it feels to be so callously betrayed, dear cousin. Prepare yourself, indeed.

CHAPTER 18

A GREAT IMPROVEMENT

"*Be not alarmed, madam, on receiving this letter, by the apprehension of its containing any repetition of those sentiments or renewal of those offers which were last night so disgusting to you.*"

Having arisen earlier than usual the next morning to the same thoughts and meditations which had at length closed her eyes and having yet to recover from the surprise of what had happened the evening before, Elizabeth had done the only thing she could do in such times as that. She escaped the parsonage without detection to indulge herself in air and exercise. Little did she know, Mr. Darcy had been of a similar mind, only he had been prepared for their encounter as evidenced by the letter he handed her. He asked her to read it, he bowed, and he immediately went on his way.

Some hours later, Elizabeth was in a fair way of memorizing everything he had said. Once again, the letter's opening resounded in her mind: *"Be not alarmed, madam, on receiving this letter, by the apprehension of its containing any repetition of those sentiments or renewal of those offers which were last night so disgusting to you."*

To have written something so eloquent, so heart-rendering, and personal, and yet so final. Would she ever really understand such a manner of man?

He had placed an extraordinary degree of faith in her character by revealing his family's most closely held secrets: how his young sister had nearly thrown herself in Mr. Wickham's power, how his own father had been blinded by Wickham's vile nature. He had disputed Wickham's lies, each one in its turn. He never denied Wickham the living in Kympton. Wickham had lied. In truth, he had refused to take orders and requested the value of the living instead. Mr. Darcy had given Mr. Wickham money, not only in this instance but time and time again.

She now perfectly remembered everything that had passed in conversation between Wickham and herself when they were walking along the path to Longbourn from Meryton some months ago. Many of his expressions were still fresh in her memory. She was now struck with the impropriety of such communications to a stranger and wondered how it had escaped her before. She saw the indelicacy of putting himself forward as he had done and realized the inconsistency of his professions with his conduct. She remembered that he had boasted of having no fear of seeing Mr. Darcy—that Mr. Darcy might leave the country, but that he should stand his ground. Yet he had avoided the Netherfield ball the very next week.

She also remembered that, till the Netherfield party had quit the country, he had told his story to none except herself; however, after their removal it had been discussed everywhere with neither reserves nor scruples in sinking Mr. Darcy's character, though he had assured her that respect for the father would always prevent his exposing the son.

How differently did everything now appear in which he was concerned.

Elizabeth grew absolutely ashamed of herself. Of neither Darcy nor Wickham could she think without feeling she had been blind, partial, prejudiced, and absurd.

How despicably I have acted! I, who have prided myself on my discernment! I, who have valued myself on my abilities to discern other people's character. Had I been in love, I could not have been more wretchedly blind! But vanity, not love, has been my folly.

Till this moment I never knew myself.

Her self-recriminations aside, there was the matter of Mr. Darcy's interference in Jane's concerns. He owed it to his obligation to his friend and entirely in the absence of any malice toward Jane. He truly believed that Jane's affections toward Mr. Bingley were in complete discordance with how they ought to be. Although Elizabeth would be the first to confess that Jane rarely showed her true feelings to anyone, she would not completely accept Mr. Darcy's explanation, insisting still that it was not his place to decide.

Some hours later when Elizabeth arrived at the parsonage house, her friend Charlotte met her at the gate. "Eliza, my dear, you will be disheartened to learn that you have just missed our morning callers."

Elizabeth supposed it was just as well, for the last thing she wanted to do on that particular morning was sit with people she barely knew and feign politeness when her mind was so busily engaged with the events of her last encounter with Mr. Darcy in the grove when he handed her the telltale letter.

Remembering herself, she said, "No doubt it was one of the parishioners calling to seek favor from Mr. Collins."

"In this case you are mistaken, for the guests I am speaking of were Mr. Darcy and Colonel Fitzwilliam."

"Mr. Darcy?" Elizabeth responded, her voice a puzzling mixture of disbelief and surprise. Having seen the unaffected look on his face earlier and having spent the next hours wandering the lanes in the wake of reading his letter, she had persuaded herself that she was the last person on earth he wished to see.

Charlotte nodded. "Yes. He and the colonel called to say goodbye before leaving for London."

"So they have left this part of the country," Elizabeth said almost in a whisper. She did not know whether she was more pleased than disappointed by this intelligence. Certainly it was a great convenience to be spared the awkwardness of seeing Mr. Darcy face to face so soon upon the heels of reading his letter. While he had promised there was to be no renewal of the sentiments that, in his words, Elizabeth had found so disgusting, a part of her whispered it would be worthwhile to express her regret for judging him so severely.

"Indeed. I suspect they had hoped to see you. In fact, the colonel made mention of walking out in search of you."

"I suppose it is just as well that he did not," she said, still quite uncertain if he had intentionally meant to sow seeds of discord between Mr. Darcy and herself. Again, she silently rebuked herself, for how could the colonel possibly have discerned any symptom of love that his cousin harbored for her when even she was caught completely unaware by his ardent love.

You must allow me to tell you how ardently I admire and love you. Even now, Elizabeth was shocked by Mr. Darcy's declaration.

"Why ever would you say that, Eliza?" Charlotte asked. "I was certain that you got along exceedingly well with both gentlemen. Surely you witnessed a great improvement in Mr. Darcy's demeanor over what it had been when we were all in Hertfordshire."

Elizabeth thought for a moment that she ought to confide all that had happened between Mr. Darcy and her with her intimate friend, and then immediately thought better of it. Not that she could not trust Charlotte with such a confidence, but she did not want her friend to think she was foolish, imprudent and even worst ridiculous. Wanting to put temptation completely aside, she said, "I suppose Phoebe was utterly delighted by the visit, even if a little disappointed to bid her favorite beau adieu—"

"Perhaps forever," Elizabeth added nostalgically after a brief pause. Now aware more than ever that Phoebe never stood a chance of garnering Mr. Darcy's affection, Elizabeth suffered a measure of pain for her cousin. Not that she suffered any guilt, for whatever had been the cause of his ardent affection was a result of no conscious act on her part.

Charlotte said, "That is the thing. You see, Phoebe did not see the gentlemen either."

"Oh? I suppose she went out for a walk." Although her cousin had never been a great walker, she had made a concerted effort to join

Elizabeth whenever she could while they were in Hunsford. Elizabeth had no doubt that the presence of a certain gentleman whom they were always meeting in the lanes was a strong inducement.

How odd that he should always turn and accompany them with such regularity. How odd the manner in which he directed so much of his attention toward her when it was evident that Phoebe was the one who went out of her way to garner his good opinion. Elizabeth was convinced that Phoebe had convinced herself that Mr. Darcy was courting her.

How odd that the gentleman believed he was courting me. Whatever I do, I must make sure that Phoebe never learns of what happened between Mr. Darcy and me since we have been here in Kent. I am sure it would break her heart to know that all of her hopes were in vain. Although I have always considered her marital scheme for the four of us to be little more than a diversion, I am not entirely certain she viewed it in the same light-hearted spirit.

Charlotte did marry Mr. Collins, after all—something Elizabeth never thought would happen. *Had it not been for the colonel, who is to say that I might have been so hasty in rejecting Mr. Darcy's hand?*

Was her own sense of right and wrong enough

to warrant the refusal of a man who professed to being ardently in love with her merely on the basis on the grievances of another man so wholly unconnected to her?

She shook her head. *The material point is I did not accept Mr. Darcy's hand, and that is the end of that.*

"No," said Charlotte, piercing Elizabeth's musings. "I have not seen her since breakfast. She asked about your whereabouts, and after I said you had gone out for a walk, she informed me that she would be in the bedroom embarking on a letter-writing campaign to her father as well as her relations in Brighton."

"Brighton? Is Phoebe planning to go away to Brighton?"

"To visit her father's relations," Charlotte said, nodding. "It appears so."

"That is rather odd. I know that she had long wanted to visit Brighton, however. But, why now?"

Charlotte shrugged. "I suppose this time in Kent has taught her to abandon the hope of winning Mr. Darcy's hand."

Feigning a lightness of heart she did not honestly feel given the events which had unfolded over the past weeks, Elizabeth said, "I suppose.

One never truly knows where affairs of the heart and possible felicity in marriage are concerned. Perhaps Phoebe has a cousin in Brighton who is in want of a wife, and she simply chose not to mention him before."

CHAPTER 19

A SIMILAR FATE

Georgiana knew she should not have listened to what was meant to be a private conversation between her brother and her cousin Colonel Fitzwilliam, but her brother had been exhibiting such odd behavior since his return from Kent. Any clues she might detect were sure to put her mind at ease. Besides, her own name had been invoked. What more license did she need to explain herself? Surely a lady's curiosity, once piqued, demanded satisfaction.

Once inside the parlor at Darcy House, Georgiana paced the floor.

She had truly believed she could rely on her brother's discretion to keep the secret of her near elopement with George Wickham to himself. She had counted upon her cousin Colonel Fitzwilliam as well. She had even relied on George Wickham himself, as well as his accomplice and her former guardian, Mrs. Younge, to guard the secret.

How alarmed she was to learn that her brother had confided her greatest secret to a stranger, someone who was so wholly unconnected to her as well as to her brother. What in the world was he thinking? Georgiana simply would not allow her companion, Mrs. Annesley, who had been studying her with a concerned eye, to know just how deeply disturbed she was by this discovery. But surely her brother would know.

I cannot wait until I see my brother.

Soon after being informed that her brother was alone in his study, Georgiana stormed into the room, surprising herself just as much as him by her severity.

"How dare you discuss my private affairs with someone so wholly unconnected to our family?" Georgiana demanded after recounting what she had heard.

Darcy's large mahogany desk was as untidy as was his physical appearance, both a consequence of the continuing tumult of his mind in the aftermath of his disastrous proposal of marriage to Miss Elizabeth. Taken aback by his younger sister's impertinence, Darcy arose from his seat. "How dare you speak to me in such a manner, young lady? Have you forgotten what you are about?"

"The least you might have done is forewarned me that you have confided my secret in others! Then I might know how to act should fate throw me in their paths."

"Georgiana, there is no harm in Miss Elizabeth Bennet knowing what happened — almost happened to you. I told her in the hopes that she might avoid a similar fate. Surely you would have done the same."

The irony of his confession was not lost on him, for he had no way of knowing whether Elizabeth had even read his letter. He prayed that she had.

"Confide my personal affairs to a casual acquaintance?" Georgiana asked. "I think not. My question stands. How could you do such a thing?"

"Miss Elizabeth is more than a casual acquaintance to me. I love her!"

And as soon as that, Georgiana's expression

changed from one of serious displeasure to one of anticipation laced with contrition. "You—you love her? Brother, I did not know. I am so sorry."

"Sorry?"

"Indeed, for rather than berating you, I feel I ought to be wishing you joy."

"No—I am afraid that will not be necessary. Not now—most likely, not ever."

"So that means you did not tell her that you love her. Is it because you are ashamed of her, owing to her lack of wealth and her lack of fortune, her family's want of connections?"

"No—yes. What I mean to say is I went to her to profess my ardent love for her in terms that hardly recommended my suit. Not only did I confess my struggles to avoid falling in love with her, owing to her lack of fortune and want of connections in comparison with my own, but I also did so with every expectation of a favorable reply."

"There is little wonder that she said no."

"Little wonder indeed."

"But, what of your heart? Have you abandoned all hope?"

"If it were merely the fact that I insulted her family, I might have a fair amount of hope, but there is more to my story than that. For one, she blames me for all of George Wickham's misfortunes."

"Is that the reason you confided in Miss Elizabeth Bennet, my secret? In order to provide evidence of George's true character."

Darcy nodded.

"But it did not work?" asked Georgiana.

He shrugged. "I can only hope she takes my words to heart, so that she and her family are spared. I should hate to think I confided in Miss Elizabeth something so critical to your reputation in vain."

"I suspect there is more than your perceived slight against Mr. Wickham that has given you reason to abandon all hope."

"There is."

"What is it, if you do not mind my asking?"

"It has to do with her sister, Miss Jane Bennet, and Charles Bingley. Miss Elizabeth believes that I am the reason that Charles did not return to Hertfordshire—that I am the cause of her sister's broken heart."

"Are you not?"

Darcy swept his fingers through his dark hair. His part in the affair in conjunction with the

Bingley sisters came to mind. He was not pleased that his sister's new friend, Miss Bingley, had discussed the matter with the younger woman, but he knew he had no one to blame but himself. Disguise of any sort was his abhorrence, and yet he had willingly taken part in the scheme to keep his friend and Miss Jane Bennet apart.

"I do not deny it. Nor did I deny it to Miss Elizabeth. I did what I did in the interest of my friend. I never believed that Miss Bennet's feelings for him were sincere. However, Miss Elizabeth's strong stance in defense of her sister has given me reason to believe that all hope for her forgiveness is lost, for as much as she loves her sister, she would never accept the man whom she believes has been the cause of subjecting her sister to derision for disappointed hopes. Those were her expressed words."

"Then, Brother, you know what you must do."

"What are you suggesting?"

"You must do everything in your power to reunite Mr. Bingley with Miss Jane Bennet."

"Georgiana, my dear, I cannot believe you would suggest such a thing. I thought—I was of the opinion that you—"

"That I wanted Mr. Bingley for myself. I will

not deny that was — nay, has long been my heart's greatest desire. But Mr. Bingley does not love me. I know you well enough to know that disguise of any sort is your abhorrence and yet you purposely resorted to a scheme to separate Mr. Bingley and Miss Bennet, which tells me that you knew he was in her power.

"If I am to be completely honest with myself, I must confess that I do not love him—not in the way I would wish to love the man with whom I am to spend the rest of my life. I suspect after what happened in Ramsgate, I was merely pacifying my wounded vanity."

"I am sorry to hear you say that, for I will not deny the prospect of an alliance between the two of you would have pleased me exceedingly."

"I know, Brother. I know. All you have ever wanted for me was that I might be happy. That is also my greatest wish for you. Now, I urge you to speak with Mr. Bingley."

CHAPTER 20

A MEASURE OF HOPE

LONDON, ENGLAND - CHEAPSIDE

Having taken Elizabeth's vehement rebuke of his officiousness in separating his friend from her sister to heart, as well as his sister's advice, Darcy sought to make amends by making his friend Bingley aware of Miss Jane Bennet's presence in town and accompanying him to Cheapside to call on her.

Seeing Miss Elizabeth upon his arrival was met with some surprise. He was certain, having heard it directly from his aunt, that Elizabeth had planned to be in Kent another fortnight at least. His aunt had also expressed her hope that Miss

Elizabeth might remain in that part of the country even longer.

The irony of his aunt's commendation of Miss Elizabeth Bennet was not lost on Mr. Darcy. How differently Lady Catherine might have behaved toward the young lady had she been presented to her ladyship as her future niece. By the manner of Elizabeth's reception, one would never have guessed that Darcy's last meeting with her in Kent had been wrought with so much contention and strife. He hoped rather than knew that his letter may have played some part in that.

Soon after all the usual civilities had been exchanged during which Mr. Darcy and Mr. Bingley had the pleasure of meeting the Bennet relations' aunt, Mrs. Gardiner, the latter suggested that the young people might enjoy a walk to the nearby park for a breath of fresh air.

With so much to say on both their parts, neither Darcy nor Bingley were inclined to object and soon enough Elizabeth and Darcy had outpaced Jane and Bingley by a considerable distance, thus allowing each couple time to talk in privacy.

"I am sorry if my being here seems untoward," said Darcy, after every topic on the weather and the park's general beauty were exhausted.

"You could not have known that I would be here. I was expected to remain in Kent for another fortnight, at least."

"You are correct," Darcy said. "I did not know you would be here, but I would be lying if I said I did not hope."

Elizabeth lowered her eyelids.

Mr. Darcy said, "Not that I mean to cause you any undue stress. As I wrote, I have no intention of repeating the avowal of that which you found so disgusting when we were together at the parsonage house."

"Sir, I wish you would not say that."

"Pardon, Miss Elizabeth?"

"It is just that words were exchanged on both our parts that perhaps would never have been spoken had a better understanding of each other's character existed. Your letter—"

"So, you did read all I have to say."

"I did. How can I apologize enough for judging you so harshly on the basis of Mr. Wickham's outright falsehoods, convenient bending of the facts, and half-truths?"

"I gave you no reason to believe otherwise. In

hindsight, I believe I ought to have been more forthcoming. This is not the first incidence of Mr. Wickham attempting to poison the hearts and minds of people against me. I dare say it will not be the last."

"Be that as it may, I ought to have been more circumspect. I have always fancied myself an excellent studier of peoples' characters."

"If I am to be completely honest, then I must apologize for my part in any misunderstandings between us. I would like to make amends."

"Is not your generosity in bringing Mr. Bingley here to Cheapside to see Jane proof of your contrition?"

"If I could do more, I most certainly would: perhaps be more open about my family's history with Mr. Wickham as a means of preventing him from further ingratiating himself and perhaps inflicting similar harm on other unsuspecting young ladies."

"I would never ask you to do that, sir. At least, not as it relates to my own family. I believe we are perfectly safe from him now that the militia has left Hertfordshire."

"I must confess that I am delighted to hear that."

Darcy and Elizabeth exchanged a look which offered the former a measure of hope. He might not have her heart, but at least he was on his way to winning her good opinion.

Whether Mr. Darcy or Elizabeth had the greater share of disappointment that their intimate intercourse was then interrupted when Jane and Bingley joined them on the lane could not be said.

The very real possibility existed that they were both suffering somewhat conflicting emotions: gladness in having taken those first steps towards eliminating any ongoing ill will and awkwardness between them pursuant to the failed proposal and anxiousness over what the next step between the two of them would be.

CHAPTER 21

CHANCE FOR HAPPINESS

*D*arcy and Bingley called on the Gardiners once again two days hence. The former's hope of a repetition of the warm reception from Miss Elizabeth was suspended upon his learning that she was not there.

Sitting in the Gardiners' parlor with Miss Bennet and his friend Bingley was rather awkward, but Darcy was determined to see Elizabeth that day. Bingley must have noticed Darcy's discomfort, and after a quarter hour had passed, he said, "What say the two of you that we go to the park for a bit of exercise and fresh air. We are certain to encounter Miss Elizabeth somewhere along the way."

"No—" Darcy said. "That is to say, I know

how eager you have been to visit Miss Bennet this morning. I shall leave you to it." He looked at Jane. "If you will pardon me, Miss Bennet, I believe I shall take my leave."

If Jane knew what Mr. Darcy's true intention was for such a hasty departure, her countenance did not reflect it. She smiled. "By all means, sir. And allow me to express my gratitude for your having come all this way to call on us. Pray you shall enjoy a lovely day."

Allowing no time for his friend to object, Darcy was gone directly.

He soon came across Elizabeth sitting on a park bench. From where he stood, she appeared to be in some distress. Mr. Darcy approached her directly, causing her to startle and spring to her feet.

"Good God! Miss Elizabeth, what is the matter? You look unwell. Shall I accompany to your uncle's home?"

"No, I thank you," she replied, endeavoring to recover herself. "There is nothing the matter with me. I am quite well. I am only worried by some dreadful news which I have just received by way of the mail."

Having said as much and likely observing his

wretched suspense mixed with compassion, she must have felt a lengthier explanation was warranted.

Her distress evident by the trembling in her voice and even her hands, she continued, "It is a letter from my cousin Phoebe. When she left Kent, she traveled to Brighton to visit her relations – her father's sister. At least that was the reason she gave, but in truth, she went there for the express purpose of throwing herself into Mr. Wickham's path."

"Wickham?"

Elizabeth nodded. "The worst part is she did so as a means of seeking revenge against me." Elizabeth lowered her head as well as her voice. "Phoebe was at the parsonage that night. She must have heard everything. Till this moment, I had no knowledge that she was there, but it seems she heard it all, and she believes my affection for Mr. Wickham is the reason for my refusal."

Elizabeth took a deep breath, hoping to slow her racing heartbeat. "What is more, she foolishly believes I ruined her chance for happiness, and she means to do the same thing to me."

"I am not following."

She turned away and looked over the nearby

pond. Its waters were so calm—a striking contrast to the tumult of her mind.

How could Phoebe be so foolish?

"I am almost embarrassed to be discussing such a sensitive subject with you, sir."

Darcy moved in front of her to command a full view of her face. "Clearly you are upset. It might help to confide in someone – to confide in me."

"It is just that Phoebe has fancied herself in love with you since the day she first laid eyes on you, sir," Elizabeth confessed, searching his face for his reaction to her speech.

"What?" Mr. Darcy asked, his expression unreadable.

"It is a long, complicated story – none of which matters now, except that I believe my cousin is on the verge of making the biggest mistake of her life."

"What exactly is she about to do, if you do not mind my asking?"

"She wrote to flaunt her *secret* engagement to Mr. Wickham. She means to elope with him to Gretna Green. You and I both know what this means. Mr. Wickham must have learned about

Phoebe's dowry, which is by no means insignificant. He intends to get his hands on her fortune.

"You know him too well to doubt the rest. His motives are completely mercenary. He does not love my cousin. I dare say he does not even care for her."

"This is grave indeed," said Darcy

"I believe I must return to Hertfordshire at once to speak with my uncle before it is too late."

"Of course. I am happy to offer my carriage if you would like – anything to assist you in your speedy return to Hertfordshire during this time of need."

"Sir, you are too generous. I do not believe that I can prevail upon you in such a manner."

The irony of her biting words of refusal struck her with force: *You are the last man in the world whom I can be prevailed on to marry.*

His face solemn, Mr. Darcy said, "You must allow me to do this for you. It is the least I can do. If I may, I would like to see you safely to your relations' home now, at which time I must make plans to leave town as well. Shall we proceed?"

Mr. Darcy and Elizabeth set off in a hurried pace with scarcely a word between them. And although the two of them were walking side by side, never before had Elizabeth felt they were so far apart. The former in earnest meditation, his brow was contracted and his air gloomy, and the latter, upon observing this, was instantly aware of what it must mean. Her power was sinking as it inevitably must sink under such a proof of family frailties and caprice.

Silent recollection of what her history had been with her walking companion could not help but intrude, adding further to her distress: his going out of his way to show kindness to her during her mishap on the way to Netherfield Park to see Jane, his preference for her, however guarded, whenever they were in company at Netherfield, his declaration of his love for her in Kent, his willingness to make amends for his part in separating Jane and Bingley, and not the least of it all, his letter which finally illustrated his true character.

Never had she so honestly felt that she could have loved him, as now, when all love must be in vain.

CHAPTER 22

A GREAT CHANGE IN SENTIMENTS

*B*ewilderment marred the elder Bennet daughter's angelic countenance as she listened to Elizabeth's speech. "I do not understand," Jane cried, once Elizabeth had finished telling her about Phoebe's fool-hearted scheme to elope with Mr. Wickham.

"I thought you always liked Mr. Wickham. Why do you find it so terribly distressing that our cousin Phoebe might like him too—dare I say love him?"

"Oh, Jane! There is so much more that has unfolded over the past weeks that has led to Phoebe's rash decision. Things I had not intended on sharing with anyone. Only Phoebe found out, and she is behaving recklessly because of it."

"Lizzy, what has happened?"

"You know how Phoebe fancied herself in love with Mr. Darcy."

"What does Mr. Darcy have to do with any of this?"

"He—" Elizabeth started, "Oh, Jane! Mr. Darcy proposed to me when we were in Kent."

Jane gasped. "Are you—are you and Mr. Darcy engaged?"

"No—no, we are not. You see, I refused him for reasons I care not to discuss, owing to their rather sensitive nature. However, it appears that Phoebe heard our entire discussion, at least the worst part of it, which I might add was most of it, for some very unpleasant words were exchanged between us. Phoebe thought my reason for rejecting Mr. Darcy's hand was because of my feelings for Mr. Wickham. She means to seek revenge against me for thwarting her chances with Mr. Darcy by thwarting my supposed chances with Mr. Wickham."

"Lizzy, I hardly know what to say. Our cousin has always been rather high spirited in nature— dare I even say impetuous. Still, I do not know why you are so distressed about the possibility of Phoebe marrying him. Is he not an honorable man, an officer, as well as a true gentleman? Surely you are not jealous of our cousin, or are you?" Jane gasped. "Lizzy! Are you in love with Mr. Wickham?"

"Heaven forbid. I believe one might safely say I detest the man."

"That is certainly a great change in sentiments towards someone who was clearly a favorite of yours for so long as he was. What has happened to alter your good opinion?"

"Suffice it to say, that I learned a great deal more about Mr. Wickham's true character while I was in Kent. I am not at liberty to go into the details, but everything I thought I knew about Mr. Wickham has been shown to be false. He is no gentleman. He is a scoundrel, one who would risk the reputation of innocent young girls solely for the purpose of gaining their fortunes.

"I have no doubt that Phoebe's dowry is Wickham's sole motivation in persuading her to elope with him. I know for a fact that our cousin would not be the first young lady to be subjected to such a scheme by Mr. Wickham's contrivances. He does not love her, and I am convinced she does not love him.

"Foolish, foolish girl. That is why it is so

important that I speak with Uncle Phillips as soon as can be, in the hope that he can put a stop to this madness before it is too late."

"I agree, and I am grateful to Mr. Darcy for making his carriage available to you, for we have not a moment to delay," said Jane, now in possession of a better appreciation of her sister's fears.

Elizabeth reached out her hand to Jane. "I regret having to tear you and Mr. Bingley apart in this manner, especially since the two of you seem well on your way to falling madly in love again."

"Lizzy, I never have been as persuaded of Mr. Bingley's affection for me as you have. These past days in company with him have been a pleasure, but I am not so convinced it can or ever will be more than that. Perhaps too much time has passed."

"Nonsense, Jane. He loves you—I only pray that what has happened does not prevent him from declaring himself to you."

"And what of you and Mr. Darcy? I know you said you rejected his proposal, and I will not pressure you into disclosing the reason for your refusal, but surely he must care for you as much as ever, else he would not have taken it upon himself to arrange our speedy return to Hertfordshire for the sake of speaking with our uncle."

"I do not know precisely why he came to our aid, but I rather suspect he feels some remorse in not having exposed Wickham when he had the chance to do so in Hertfordshire, for had he, then none of this would have happened. I would not have so willingly bestowed Mr. Wickham my good opinion, and by extension, my highest commendations, and Phoebe would not have thrown herself in his path with the intention of wounding me."

Jane shrugged. "I do not know, Lizzy. A part of me suspects Mr. Darcy's intentions are more generous than that."

"Jane, what are you saying? Surely you do not believe Mr. Darcy is still in love with me and that is why he has been so helpful."

"Do you not?"

It was now Elizabeth's turn to shrug. "Even if a part of me suspected such a thing, surely it no longer signifies. If you could but have seen his face when we parted. He looked as though he could not wait to get away from me, and why would he not in the face of my family's deficits? In so many ways, Phoebe is more like a sister to me than even Mary, Kitty, and Lydia. Anyone who knows either of us is very aware there is no denying our connection, nor would I ever wish it."

I fear whatever my wishes might be, Mr. Darcy is lost to me forever.

CHAPTER 23

ALL THE USUAL CIVILITIES

Though saddened by the thought of what more time in London might have meant for her sister Jane as well as herself, Elizabeth was not designed for ill humor. Upon her arrival home, she dared not delay visiting her Meryton relations for fear of being too late to save her cousin from her own impetuous self. There she sat across from Mr. and Mrs. Phillips, her letter inside her pocket if needed as corroboration of her story.

"No, we have not heard from our dear Phoebe for quite a while," Mrs. Phillips replied when Elizabeth broached the topic after all the usual civilities were exchanged. "But you know how your cousin is. She never has any time to write. She is always so happily engaged in meeting new people. I understand that Brighton can be quite diverting at this particular time of the year, especially with the militia being there. You are aware that the militia went to Brighton when they left Meryton, are you not?"

Elizabeth said, "Oh, yes, of course, I am very aware. That is precisely the reason for my being here. Dear Uncle and Aunt Phillips, prepare yourself for something dreadful, for you see, I have recently received a letter from my cousin Phoebe. I am quite devastated by what she has to say, and when you hear it for yourselves, I am sure you will be equally devastated."

"Pray, Lizzy, how dare you keep us in suspense? What does our dear Phoebe have to say?"

Elizabeth asked that both of her relations take a seat, although she chose to pace the floor as, line by line, she recounted to her aunt and uncle what Phoebe had said—that she had gotten herself engaged to be married to Mr. Wickham.

What happened next stunned Elizabeth. To say that Mrs. Phillips was ecstatic would be a great understatement.

While it was true that it was every young

woman's greatest wish to be happily married, it was also true that the young lady ought to be sensible in her choice when she was able to be so, and certainly Phoebe, with all of her manifold attractions as well as her handsome dowry was more than capable of attracting a gentleman of consequence.

How her mother could be happy about the prospect of her only child finding herself engaged to be married to a man of Mr. Wickham's low character, Elizabeth could not fathom.

Of course, my aunt and uncle do not know him as I do. Dare I confide in them all that Mr. Darcy told me in the hopes that they might be persuaded to prevent their daughter from making what would undoubtedly prove to be the biggest mistake of her life? I feel I must say something.

"I do not believe that this course of action that Phoebe has chartered for herself is a wise one," Elizabeth heard herself say. Steeling her voice with resolve, she continued, "I know with certainty that she does not truly care for Mr. Wickham—not in the way that a young lady ought to care for the man with whom she plans to spend the rest of her life."

"How do you know, Miss Lizzy?" Mrs. Phillips asked. "Unless I am mistaken, the last time I saw you, you were more than a little enamored by Mr. Wickham's charms. In fact, I believe with all my heart had his head not been turned by Miss King, then surely you would not have surrendered him so easily as you did. Who is to say that you are not simply jealous of my Phoebe?"

"It is interesting that you mentioned Miss King, for I am sure you are more than aware that she was sent to Liverpool by her family as a means of protecting her. I have it on good authority, you see, that Mr. Wickham is mercenary. Not only did he attempt to gain Miss King's fortune in return for the promise of future felicity, the likes of which he is quite incapable, but he has done it before to another wealthy young lady.

"No doubt, Phoebe's dowry of ten thousand pounds is his inducement once again." She looked at her uncle intently. "That is why I have come to you. I implore you to do what you can to put a stop to this. Please go to Brighton or, at the very least, notify your relations in Brighton of Mr. Wickham's bad reputation, so that they might exercise whatever measures are necessary to protect Phoebe."

Elizabeth talked on in this way until finally, she began to see that despite her attempts to reason with her aunt, who behaved as ridiculously as a mother with a single daughter in want of a husband might be expected to conduct herself, she believed that she had reasoned successfully with Mr. Phillips. Walking with her to the door, her uncle gave her every assurance that he had heard what she said and that her efforts in coming to him had not been in vain.

This was enough said for Elizabeth to leave her relations' house with some sense of comfort that she had done all she could to help Phoebe escape the unhappy fate she had charted for herself. The rest was in the hands of others who were far more powerful than she.

I only hope that whatever is to be done to save my cousin is done swiftly. And although I know Phoebe may likely despise me for my part in the scheme, I truly believe that someday she will thank me.

CHAPTER 24

THE BIGGEST MISTAKE

Though it had taken a while, Mrs. Bennet had finally come to terms with the fact that Mr. Bingley might never propose to her dear Jane, having learned from her sister Mrs. Gardiner that the young man had called upon Jane in Cheapside at least two times before Jane's abrupt leave-taking of London to return to Longbourn.

Mrs. Bennet had also learned that Mr. Darcy had accompanied his friend on both occasions. She could only attribute it to the fact that the haughty man had always taken such prodigious care of Mr. Bingley and in coming with him to Cheapside, this was no different. Not once did she consider that Mr. Darcy may have had another purpose in accompanying his friend. Why would she? Mrs. Bennet never really liked Mr. Darcy, and she had no reason to suppose that a man of his proud nature would be interested in either of her daughters, especially Elizabeth.

If Elizabeth could take but one small consolation in seeing a normal routine settling over their lives, it was that her cousin Phoebe had returned home from Brighton, a single woman. For whatever reason, her cousin was now safe from Mr. Wickham.

Elizabeth suspected rather than knew that she had her uncle Mr. Phillips to thank for saving Phoebe from the gentleman, but she could have no real way of knowing, for the entire matter had been settled in such a hushed-up manner. Other than Elizabeth, Jane, Mr. Phillips and Mrs. Phillips, no one in the neighborhood ever knew that Phoebe had fancied herself engaged to the officer. Otherwise, the matter could not possibly have been settled so quietly and so expeditiously as it had been.

Phoebe, of course, knew, and she knew that Elizabeth knew. When the two cousins were together on that particular day with no one else about to hear what they were discussing, Phoebe said, "I suppose you are wondering why I did not go through with the marriage to *your* Mr. Wickham?"

Elizabeth said, "*My* Mr. Wickham? I believe you are the one who wrote to me boasting of your engagement, did you not?"

"I did indeed, and as you might as well know, I never truly intended to go so far as to marry him. I simply meant to make it impossible that the two of you might ever enjoy the privilege."

Crossing one arm over the other, Elizabeth declared, "Then, I find myself in your debt, for Mr. Wickham is indeed the last man in the world to whom I would have ever wished to be married."

Raising her hand to her chin, Phoebe commenced tapping with her finger. "Let me think; when have I heard you express those words before?" Feigning astonishment, she cried, "Oh! I remember. It was when you uttered those words or words of a similar vein to poor Mr. Darcy."

Elizabeth tossed a quick glance over her shoulder to make sure that her cousin's speech had not been overheard. "Pray lower your voice, Phoebe. I do not believe I shall ever forgive you for not making your presence known that evening at the parsonage and for your having listened purposely to a conversation that you knew was meant to be solely between two people."

She placed her hand on her cousin's arm. "That is beside the point now, for I must ask you to keep what you heard a secret. My mother will never forgive me should she learn the truth. Surely you cannot hate me so much as to wish such a fate as my mother's endless vexation and consternation against me."

Phoebe shrugged. "I do not hate you at all, even though I really should, for you knew that I had singled Mr. Darcy out as my future husband. It was wrong of you to lead him on as you did only to break his heart."

"Lead him on? Break his heart? I did neither of those things." Forcing herself to remain calm, Elizabeth added, "I had no idea that Mr. Darcy was in love with me until he offered his hand in marriage."

Hearing this, Phoebe rolled her eyes. Though she uttered not a single word, her silence spoke volumes.

Elizabeth exclaimed, "Oh! Why am I defending myself to you? You have always believed whatever you chose to believe, and there is no reason to suppose that will ever change."

Indeed, in so many ways, Phoebe was very much like Elizabeth's youngest sister, Lydia: spoiled and prone to act without thinking or caring about the consequences of such behavior. *Of course, as the only child of an uncouth mother, what else might one expect?*

Continuing her speech, Elizabeth said, "I only ask that you keep what you overheard a secret. You are my cousin. Do I ask too much?"

Phoebe scoffed. "Oh, of course, I shall keep your secret, even though I really should be extremely vexed at you. But none of that matters anymore. You stole Mr. Darcy away from me, and I stole Mr. Wickham from you. And now we are even."

Now it was Elizabeth's turn to scoff. "So long as you promise not to tell anyone what you heard or rather thought you heard, you may think whatever you wish. Saying that, I am only glad that you came to your senses before making the biggest mistake of your life."

"La! I find it entirely ironic that you are overjoyed that I did not make what you consider might have been the biggest mistake of my life when you would have me keep your secret regarding your making the biggest mistake of your own life."

"The biggest mistake of my life? What on earth do you mean? What mistake have I made?"

"Dearest Cousin, if you do not consider refusing the hand of a man of Mr. Darcy's consequence, a man who declared his ardent love for you, the biggest mistake of your life, then I believe I never really knew you at all."

CHAPTER 25

SUCH A NOTION

"Oh, Mr. Bennet! Mr. Bennet, have you heard the news?" said his lady to him that day.

"If you are referring to the news that young Mr. Bingley has returned to Netherfield, then yes, I have heard the news, and let me just say before you ask: no, I will not call on that young man again. He knows where we live, and unless I am mistaken, he knows he is indebted to come and have a family dinner with us. Is that not correct?"

"Indeed, it is, and I am sure he will come this time."

"Oh? How can you be so sure?"

"You know very well Mr. Bingley called on our Jane when she was in London. I posit that he simply wanted more time before offering his hand in marriage and now he has returned to Netherfield, prepared to do what he ought to have done months ago." She clasped her hands and rested them against her bosom. "Oh, what a happy day this is. What a happy day indeed!"

Elizabeth then walked into the room. "Dare I ask what the reason for such jubilation is?"

"Owe it to the imminent return of the amiable Mr. Bingley," replied Mr. Bennet before his lady could fashion a response to Elizabeth's question. "Your mother is of the opinion that the sole reason for the gentleman's return is to offer his hand in marriage to your sister Jane."

"What other possible reason is there?" Mrs. Bennet asked.

"There is the small matter of his having let Netherfield Park," Elizabeth replied, throwing a teasing glance at her father. "Is the gentleman not allowed to return to his own home with impunity?"

"Impunity! What utter nonsense, Lizzy. How can you talk so? You know very well how much Mr. Bingley loves our dear Jane."

"Who is to say what Mr. Bingley thinks or how he feels?" Mr. Bennet opined. "I understand that both Jane and Lizzy had the pleasure of receiving the gentleman when they were in town. I suspect that the young man is not the most constant lover. Perhaps all the affections you suppose ought to be reserved for Jane have since been transferred to my Lizzy."

As much as Elizabeth was wont to admire her father's tendency to make sport of others, even her own mother and sisters at times, she was not so pleased by this particular conjecture. Of course, she could not be too aggrieved by her father's jest. He could have no way of knowing that Phoebe blamed Elizabeth for Mr. Darcy's supposed defection.

"How absurd! But then again, what more am I to expect? You are always giving Lizzy the preference."

"So long as you gain a son-in-law, what does it matter which of our two eldest daughters he marries?"

"Oh! Mr. Bennet, how can you abuse your own children in such a way? You take delight in vexing me. You have no compassion for my poor nerves. Besides, Mr. Bingley was not alone when he called on Jane in Cheapside. His friend Mr. Darcy was with him—although, for the life of me,

I cannot understand why or even how that came to be."

She huffed. "Imagine that! The proud Mr. Darcy at such a place as Cheapside. No doubt, having gone there, he hardly considered a month's ablutions enough to cleanse him from its impurities. And to think, he did so not just once, but twice. You might just as well have accused him of being in love with Lizzy."

Hearing her mother speak so derisively about a man whose character she scarcely understood pained Elizabeth, but she kept her silence.

Mr. Bennet, however, did not. Folding his paper and standing in preparation to quit the room, he laughed out loud. "Now, such a notion as that would indeed be absurd."

The next day or so, Elizabeth silently chastised herself. She knew she should not have been listening to what was meant to be a private conversation between her father and her uncle Mr. Phillips, especially after her stern rebuke to her cousin Phoebe mere days before for eavesdropping, but the mentioning of Mr. Darcy's name had practically stopped her in her tracks.

Standing just outside the partly opened door of her father's study, Elizabeth overheard the following:

"Surely if Mr. Bingley's friend Mr. Darcy accompanies him to Netherfield, I ought to call on the gentleman to thank him properly for his part in saving my Phoebe from that detestable Mr. Wickham. What a scoundrel he turned out to be, did he not?"

Elizabeth had nearly gasped aloud. She could not help but draw a little closer and listen to more of what her father and her uncle had to say. This improved vantage point also offered a glimpse inside the room, and she espied the two gentlemen standing by the fireplace.

Mr. Bennet nodded. "I must confess Mr. Wickham did a fine job of making love to all of us. I am surely thankful that young Lydia fell ill soon after I was cajoled into allowing her to travel with the head of the militia, Colonel Forster, and his young bride to Brighton, else I might have found myself in dire need of Mr. Darcy's intervention."

"Then you agree that I ought to thank him in person."

His brow arched, Mr. Bennet replied, "I do not know that I am saying that at all. You did say that when he went to your brother in Brighton, offering to be of service to him in preventing Phoebe from making what would have been a grave mistake, Mr. Darcy did so under the condition of anonymity. I dare say he would not wish for such an acknowledgment. One never knows why these proud men behave as they do. Perhaps such magnanimity is simply the fashion."

Elizabeth had heard enough. She could hardly believe a word she had heard.

Why would Mr. Darcy travel all the way to Brighton to save my cousin from Mr. Wickham? He and Phoebe are not strangers to each other to be sure, but their connection is hardly one of any consequence. Surely he does not have a habit of being of service to every young woman in danger from Mr. Wickham.

A part of her could not help but suppose that he had done it all for her, but did she dare presume so much?

She had to know. And she would know even if it meant asking him herself. But when?

Her uncle's speculation that Mr. Darcy might

accompany Mr. Bingley to Hertfordshire soon became Elizabeth's favorite wish that he indeed would. Not that she supposed any explicitly proffered gratitude on her part might lead to a repetition of his professions of love.

"Be not alarmed, madam, on receiving this letter, by the apprehension of its containing any repetition of those sentiments or renewal of those offers which were last night so disgusting to you. I write without any intention of paining you or humbling myself by dwelling on wishes which, for the happiness of both, cannot be too soon forgotten."

Those words were etched in her memory. Nonetheless, any ensuing improvement of his good opinion was something that she desired very much.

CHAPTER 26

AN EQUAL MEASURE OF DISCRETION

"I have come to learn the most dreadful things about Mr. Wickham. It seems his misdeeds caught up with him in Brighton, and he has abandoned the militia. His whereabouts are completely unknown. Who knew he was such a vile creature who had amassed a considerable amount of debt, mostly gambling, mind you, in his wake?

"Thank heavens, you were persuaded to come to your senses before you actually married the man," said Mrs. Phillips to her daughter upon finding her sitting alone in the parlor, staring mindlessly out the window. "I should hate to imagine what our friends and neighbors would now think of us—to say nothing of my sister

Bennet. We would be the subject of the most severe censure imaginable."

Phoebe recalled Wickham having spoken of his urgency to be away from Brighton and its being the catalyst for her silly elopement scheme. She had neither seen nor heard from him since, which suited her perfectly well.

"Oh, Mama! I was never really in love with Mr. Wickham. I only pretended to be in order to exact an act of fitting revenge against Cousin Lizzy after she stole Mr. Darcy away from me."

"Pray, do not be absurd, my child. Everyone who knows anything at all knows that Lizzy does not even like that gentleman—with all of his fancy airs and even if he does have ten thousand pounds a year."

"Which is precisely the reason I felt so betrayed. Cousin Lizzy never liked him because she was always in love with Mr. Wickham, but that did not stop her from using her feminine arts and allurements to her best advantage to turn Mr. Darcy's head."

"You know your cousin would never do such a thing."

"Then why in heaven's name, pray tell, would he have asked her to marry him?" Phoebe drew in a deep breath, for she knew what happened in Hunsford was meant to be a great secret. She had promised her cousin as much.

"Mr. Darcy asked our Lizzy to marry him? Oh, wait until I see my sister! How dare she keep such happy news a secret when everyone knows the business of her life is to marry off her five daughters? Oh, why in heavens would she keep such a thing a secret? He has ten thousand pounds a year! Why, he is as good as a lord!"

"No, Mama! You must not say a word. I should not have said a word."

"But why should news this exciting remain a secret?"

"Lizzy is not engaged to Mr. Darcy."

"But you just said he proposed to her."

"I did, and he did. But Lizzy refused his hand and in such terms as to ensure there will never be a repetition of his proposal even if he does fancy her so much, for what man would dare offer his hand in marriage to a woman who has already refused him once?"

Mrs. Phillips shook her head.

"Leave it to Lizzy to refuse the one man who might have been the means of saving her family from desolation should my brother Bennet die—

which he most certainly will, for everyone must die sooner or later.

"Indeed, it was selfish enough on her part to have refused Mr. Collins's offer of marriage, but there can be no reasonable explanation at all for her rejecting Mr. Darcy's hand. Is there any wonder she would wish for such foolish behavior to be kept a secret? My sister would be positively livid were she to find out. I dare say even her own father would frown on such foolishness.

"I will do my best to keep it a secret although I cannot promise you anything, but I will promise you that I will try to keep your secret and that is about the best I can do." Donning her bonnet and shawl, Mrs. Phillips headed toward the door.

"Mama, where are you going?"

"Why, to Longbourn Village of course. I have neither seen nor heard from my sister in days, and I miss her terribly. I shall not be away for very long."

"But you will not tell my aunt about Lizzy's secret, I pray. You kept my so-called engagement a secret, after all. Surely you can afford an equal measure of discretion where Lizzy's secret is concerned."

"Heavens, Daughter! Do not be ridiculous.

Your so-called engagement was nothing at all in comparison to what your cousin has done. Your behavior might well have been deemed scandalous, whereas Lizzy's behavior is a symptom of utter madness," cried Mrs. Phillips.

And with these words she hastily left the room, and Phoebe heard her mother the next moment open the front door and quit the house.

Upon entering Longbourn House, Mrs. Phillips espied her sister, Mrs. Bennet, and the two youngest Bennet daughters with their ears firmly pressed against the closed parlor door.

"What are you listening to?" she asked, rushing to secure her place beside the others.

"Hush," whispered Mrs. Bennet, waving her sister away with her dainty lace handkerchief.

"Why? Who is inside?"

Mrs. Bennet sighed heavily and, surrendering her place, took her sister by the arm, and coaxed her away from the door.

"It is Mr. Bingley and my Jane." Mrs. Bennet's eyes were full of unshed tears of joy. "Oh! Sister, we are saved. Mr. Bingley is asking Jane to marry him as we speak!"

Mrs. Phillips' eyes opened wide. "Well, aren't you a lucky woman, dear Sister? Two daughters engaged to wealthy gentlemen with hardly any trouble at all to yourself."

"What nonsense, Sister! I said my Jane is going to be engaged. I said nothing at all about any of my other girls."

"Then, you really do not know, do you?"

"Know what?"

Mrs. Phillips looked back at the door. By now Mary had also joined her sisters and had taken up the task of spying on the eldest sister as well.

"Where is Lizzy?"

"Oh! Who knows? Who even cares? Jane is about to become the mistress of Netherfield. I always said she could not be so beautiful for nothing."

"Yes, and you also said Lizzy is clever. Of course, once you have heard what I have to say, you might have cause to reconsider."

"Lizzy? Clever? Headstrong and obstinate is more like it. Pray, Sister, what in heavens are you trying so hard to tell me?"

"I really think you ought to be seated when

you hear what I have to say," said the other woman, attempting to coax her sister farther away from the parlor door.

"But what about Jane? What about Mr. Bingley? I dare not miss my chance to be among the first to congratulate them. What if he should change his mind?"

"You will be wishing the two of them joy soon enough. By the bye, I was given to believe his friend Mr. Darcy accompanied him from town."

Her manner ill-tempered, Mrs. Bennet exclaimed, "Oh! That horrible Mr. Darcy! He had the audacity to come here with Mr. Bingley. But he went away soon enough to allow Mr. Bingley time to request a private audience with Jane. He could not have quit Longbourn soon enough for my taste."

Still coaxing her sister along to another room, Mrs. Phillips said, "I wager you will not feel that way once you hear what I have to say."

"For heaven's sake, do not keep me in suspense a second longer. Say what you came here to say or I shall go distracted."

All too aware of what was likely unfolding inside Longbourn House, Elizabeth sat alone on a bench just off the gravel walk that led to the copse. Seeing her mother's appalling lack of decorum as the two gentlemen from Netherfield, Mr. Bingley and Mr. Darcy, entered the paddock had sent her fleeing the parlor before they were shown into the room. She knew and understood that she would see Mr. Darcy sooner or later. Indeed, she wanted to see him if for nothing else than to thank him for what he had done for her cousin. For the time being, she simply wanted more time to compose herself.

She was roused from her seat and her reflections, by someone's approach and the next thing she knew, her cousin Phoebe was standing before her.

"Cousin Lizzy, I am so glad I found you before it is too late," the younger woman cried, her breathing labored.

"Too late? Too late for what?"

"Well, it has to do with Mama who is at Longbourn, as we speak, visiting your mother. Oh! Lizzy, I am ever so sorry. Please say you will forgive me."

"Phoebe!" Elizabeth exclaimed. "What did you do?"

"First, you must promise to forgive me."

Suspecting the worse, Elizabeth said, "Phoebe! Tell me anything except that you told someone what happened in Kent between Mr. Darcy and me!"

Her voice filled with contrition, Phoebe explained what she had done. At length, she cried, "Dearest Lizzy, how can I make amends? Tell me what is to be done, and it shall be done."

"I think you have done quite enough," said Elizabeth, turning on her heels rather abruptly in order to escape her cousin before she said something she might regret.

Why did I ever believe Phoebe could be relied on to keep such a secret?

"Where are you going?" Phoebe asked.

"To Longbourn, of course, in the hopes of mitigating the damage wrought by your loose tongue."

Elizabeth was gone directly, leaving her cousin standing there. Utterly speechless.

CHAPTER 27

SO MATERIAL A CHANGE

*E*lizabeth did not walk very far before espying Mr. Darcy just up ahead. The urgency in his steps upon seeing her gave her cause to be alarmed.

Did he know that his proposal to her was now a matter of public knowledge? And if he did, did he hate her?

She needed to know.

"Mr. Darcy," said Elizabeth when the two of them were standing face-to-face.

"Miss Elizabeth," he replied, bowing. "I have just left your home. Meeting you like this is a welcome surprise."

By the looks of things, he did not know. At least he did not know yet. And for that, Elizabeth was grateful. It would not do for him to hear of Phoebe's lapse from another, and thus Elizabeth seized the chance to tell him herself.

"Sir, I do not know any way to tell you, other than to come right out and say it and hope that you will not be too disgusted."

"This sounds very serious, Miss Elizabeth. What is it?"

"It seems—well, sir, it seems—"

"Miss Elizabeth, I should like to think by now that you and I are comfortable being frank with each other."

"I have every reason to suspect that my mother has learned of your proposal of marriage to me."

His countenance clouded with concern, Darcy said nothing, which was sufficient encouragement for Elizabeth to continue.

"I already told you that my cousin Phoebe overheard the entirety of our conversation that evening at the parsonage, and while she assured me that she would not breathe a word of it to anyone, I fear making such a promise was far easier than keeping it. Phoebe told her mother, who has very likely told my mother. You know all the parties concerned too well not to know what this means. Oh! Sir, this is dreadful. How I wish I could make amends, for I fear your reputation is about to be torn into tatters."

"Things need not be as hopeless as that, Miss Elizabeth."

"Sir?"

"I proposed to you because I wanted you to be my wife. Nothing has happened since then that has changed that fact.

"Despite what I said in the letter which, in hindsight, I must confess was the product of my severely bruised ego–that there would be no repetition of the sentiments avowed when I proposed–I find myself standing here before you today telling you that you have bewitched me body and soul. I love you. If your feelings have changed towards me—if you can find it in your heart to forgive me for my ungentlemanly like proposal, then I ask you once again. Please do me the honor of accepting my hand in marriage."

The anxiety of their situation compelled Elizabeth to speak, and she immediately gave him to understand that her sentiments had undergone so material a change since their time together in Kent as to make her receive his proposal of marriage with gratitude and indeed great pleasure.

The happiness which this reply produced was exactly as it ought to be, and Mr. Darcy expressed himself on the occasion as sensibly and as warmly as a man violently in love can be supposed to do.

His longing, his affection, and all his hopes and dreams for their future felicity where tenderly conveyed when his lips touched her lips for the very first time, proving just how much she was loved by him.

At length, the newly betrothed couple walked on, without knowing in what direction. There was too much to be thought, and felt, and said, for attention to any other objects. Being a curious creature, it was imperative that Elizabeth find out precisely what Mr. Darcy's role had been in the Brighton affair. As his explanation was perfectly reasonable, Elizabeth thanked him for what he had done on her cousin's behalf.

As neither of the young lovers was in a hurry to face the reception which no doubt awaited them at Longbourn, they continued walking. After accounting for the reasons that Mr. Darcy fell in love with her, Elizabeth wanted to know what the feelings of those who meant the most to him, specifically his sister, Miss Georgiana Darcy, would be upon learning of the engagement.

Mr. Darcy said, "I had written of you many times before when we were together in Hertfordshire as well as made mention of the fact that you were visiting your friend Mrs. Collins at Easter. I feel it is also incumbent on me to tell you that Georgiana is aware of my telling you of her unfortunate experience with Mr. Wickham."

"Oh, dear," cried Elizabeth, "Pray she does not suffer any ill-will toward you for telling me or toward me for now knowing that which was meant to be a closely held family secret."

"In truth, she was quite upset upon learning what I had done, but once I made her aware of all the particulars, she was quite eager to wish me joy. In hearing that her felicitations were in vain, she was adamant that I must do everything in my power to make amends. She has always wanted a sister, and now that one of her fondest wishes is about to come true, I wager four sides of paper will be insufficient to contain all her delight and all her earnest desire of being loved by you."

"And what of Lady Catherine de Bourgh? What do you suppose her reaction will be upon learning that her favorite nephew has chosen a bride?" Elizabeth did not wish to elaborate on the rumor that he was supposedly engaged to marry his cousin Miss Anne de Bourgh. There would be time enough for such talk in the days and weeks to come.

"I have little doubt that my aunt Lady Catherine will be rendered exceedingly angry upon hearing of our engagement. On a happier note, having met the colonel, you can have no doubt of his reception."

Elizabeth nodded. "Yes, that is because the colonel is such an amiable man who makes friends wherever he goes. But what of his father and mother, Lord and Lady Matlock? Will they be just as severe as Lady Catherine?"

"While it is true that both of them may have been harboring the hope that I would choose a bride from among the *ton*, I have to believe that they will welcome you into our family with open arms. Although Lady Catherine is the earl's sister, their temperaments are entirely dissimilar."

"That is good to know," Elizabeth exclaimed, her spirits playful. "Everyone must look forward to at least a little support from their future relations."

"And what of your own family? Judging by the

relief that shone on your mother's face when I took my leave of Longbourn earlier today, she will suffer some measure of disappointment."

Elizabeth laughed a little at his conjecture. "Disappointment, Mr. Darcy? If you believe that, then you have not been paying attention to my mother at all."

"Then, you are saying she will be pleased?" Mr. Darcy asked, reaching out and caressing Elizabeth's chin with his finger.

Thoughts of what her mother's effusions might be danced through Elizabeth's mind: *"Good gracious! Lord bless me! Only think! Dear me! Mr. Darcy! Who would have thought it! Oh! My sweetest Lizzy! How rich and how great you will be! What pin-money, what jewels, what carriages you will have!*

"I am so pleased—so happy. Such a charming man! So handsome! So tall! Oh, my dear Lizzy! Pray, apologize for my having disliked him so much before. I hope he will overlook it.

"Dear, dear Lizzy. A house in town! Everything that is charming! Ten thousand pounds a year! Oh, Lord! What will become of me? I shall go distracted."

Elizabeth pursed her lips amid these reflections. *What an embarrassment it would be should my mother greet our arrival with such exaltations as this.*

"My mother will surely be as pleased with the news as a mother of five daughters in want of husbands can expect to be."

"Does the same apply to your father?" Mr. Darcy asked.

Elizabeth could also imagine what her father's reaction might be: "*Lizzy, what are you doing? Are you out of your senses to be accepting this man? Have not you always disliked him? He is rich, to be sure, and you may have many fine clothes and fine carriages. But will that make you happy?*"

Not that she would be too concerned, for despite wishing her former opinions had been more reasonable, her expressions more moderate, she was confident that an earnest profession of her current sentiments was all that would be required to persuade her father of her sincerest attachment to Mr. Darcy.

Leaving out the first part, Elizabeth told Mr. Darcy as much. To complete the favorable impression of her family's anticipated joy, Elizabeth remarked on the pleasure her uncle and aunt Mr. and Mrs. Gardiner would enjoy upon learning of the engagement as well.

It was thus decided that everyone who mattered most to the two of them would be overjoyed by the news of the engagement, and the sentiments of those who were wont to suffer displeasure, specifically the Miss Bingleys of the world, could have no impact at all on the future Mr. and Mrs. Darcy's felicity.

CHAPTER 28

COMFORT AND ELEGANCE

The news that Elizabeth had accepted Mr. Darcy's proposal was met with all the excitement and jubilation that could be expected. Amid all the confusion brought about by two engagements, Elizabeth was anxious to make time for her dearest sister.

"I am certainly one of the most fortunate creatures that ever existed!" cried Jane. "Oh! Lizzy, to know you too are equally blessed means the world to me."

Elizabeth smiled as warmly as could be expected. "Dearest Jane, you cannot know what it means to me to see you so happy. I believe I shall love your Mr. Bingley almost as much as I love Mr. Darcy."

Jane and Elizabeth merely giggled at this conjecture.

"Oh, Lizzy, I beg you to be serious, for I must know how it came to be that you left Longbourn with little to no discernible prospect for felicity in marriage in the foreseeable future and you returned engaged to marry Mr. Darcy. What is more, why ever did Mama act as though your engagement was a foregone conclusion?"

"In a word," Elizabeth began, "Phoebe."

"Phoebe?"

"Indeed, Phoebe," Elizabeth replied. "Suffice it to say, the entire affair is a rather tangled web. But fear not, for I shall tell you everything there is to know in due time. For now, I suggest you take your place by your Mr. Bingley's side. By the looks of it, he is desperately missing you."

"As you will no doubt take your place by your Mr. Darcy's side," Jane said knowingly.

Smiling, Elizabeth said, "*My* Mr. Darcy. I think I like the sound of that."

With two daughters engaged in one day, Mrs. Bennet was a happy woman indeed. On such an auspicious occasion as this, little wonder she was able to have a gathering that very evening which included family and close friends and her two future sons-in-law as guests of honor. The Phillipses were sure to be there, and when Phoebe could, she went to Elizabeth and embraced her.

"Cousin Lizzy, allow me to be among the first to wish you joy. I declare you are the luckiest of us all, for not only is your future husband rich, but he is also handsome, which, as I recall, ranked at the very top of your list of what a future husband ought to be."

"Pray, Phoebe, lower your voice!" Elizabeth scolded, thankful that no one was standing close enough to hear what was being said. She could well imagine the parading, the obsequious civility and indeed the vulgarity that might well tax her future husband's forbearance during their season of courtship. How delightfully different their lives would be once they were removed from such society to the comfort and elegance of Pemberley.

"Do not tell me you are angry with me for telling your secret," Phoebe cried.

Throwing a casual glance about the room, Elizabeth said nothing in response, which was sufficient encouragement for her cousin to continue pressing her point.

"I am not saying Mr. Darcy might never have proposed to you again, but you have to confess a part of you feared no gentleman would likely propose twice to the same woman. Had I held my tongue, you might not be standing here before me this evening as the future Mrs. Fitzwilliam Darcy."

Much too pleased with the way things had unfolded to be really angry, Elizabeth laughed a little at this conjecture. "So, you are suggesting I ought to be thanking you."

The other young lady nodded. "Indeed, you should be thanking me, for in confiding your secret, I like to suppose I have been the means of uniting you and Mr. Darcy."

"Phoebe, you credit yourself for what was merely a confluence of favorable events."

"Oh! Cousin Lizzy, you are no fun at all. You won the greatest prize of all in our little scheme. As it was my idea from the start, can I not claim even a little share of your felicity?"

"Won what prize?" Darcy asked as he approached the two cousins and took his place by Elizabeth's side.

The very sight of him made Elizabeth's heart race. The remembrance of the liberties she had allowed him when the two of them were alone some hours earlier made it skip a beat.

Elizabeth said, "I am afraid it is a long story and one that I will gladly share with you at a more convenient time. Suffice it to say that my cousin Phoebe, despite failing to hold her tongue as she promised me she would, congratulates herself instead for being the means of uniting the two of us. She insists I ought to be thanking her."

Mr. Darcy took Elizabeth's hand and raised it to his lips. Lowering her hand, he looked at Phoebe. "Then, let me express our mutual gratitude to you, Miss Phillips."

Phoebe beamed with pleasure in acknowledgment of Mr. Darcy's gallantry. "You see, Cousin Lizzy, Mr. Darcy bears me no ill-will. You could learn a great deal from your future husband on the power of forgiveness."

When Phoebe was gone, Darcy said, "That was interesting. I can hardly wait to hear more of this prize your cousin spoke of before. Perhaps you might join me outside for a rather lengthy private intercourse."

Smiling, Elizabeth said, "I should be delighted

to join you anywhere your heart desires for a *lengthy* private intercourse, sir, but only on one condition."

"And what is that?"

"Talk of anything having to do with my cousin must be the last thing that crosses our lips."

Leaning as close as propriety allowed in a room full of people and speaking in a manner meant solely for Elizabeth's ears, Darcy said, "With lips as tender and sweet as yours, my dearest, loveliest Elizabeth, I am more than happy to oblige."

ALSO BY P. O. DIXON

Standalone

Gravity

Which that Season Brings

Designed for Each Other

Irrevocably Gone

By Reason, by Reflection, by Everything

Impertinent Strangers

Bewitched, Body and Soul

To Refuse Such a Man

Miss Elizabeth Bennet

Still a Young Man

Love Will Grow

Only a Heartbeat Away

As Good as a Lord

Matter of Trust

Almost Persuaded

Series

Everything Will Change
Lady Elizabeth
So Far Away

Dearest, Loveliest Elizabeth
Dearest Elizabeth
Loveliest Elizabeth
Dearest, Loveliest Elizabeth

A Darcy and Elizabeth Love Affair
A Lasting Love Affair
'Tis the Season for Matchmaking

Pride and Prejudice Untold
To Have His Cake (and Eat it Too)
What He Would Not Do
Lady Harriette

Darcy and the Young Knight's Quest
He Taught Me to Hope
The Mission
Hope and Sensibility

Darcy and Elizabeth Short Stories

A Night with Mr. Darcy to Remember

Expecting His Proposal

Pride and Sensuality

A Tender Moment

* * *

Visit http://podixon.com for more.

ABOUT THE AUTHOR

P. O. Dixon is a writer as well as an entertainer. Historical England and its days of yore fascinate her. She, in particular, loves the Regency period with its strict mores and oh so proper decorum. Her ardent appreciation of Jane Austen's timeless works set her on the writer's journey.

FEATURED BOOK EXCERPT

Twitter: @podixon
Facebook: facebook.com/podixon
Website: podixon.com
Newsletter: bit.ly/SuchHappyNews
Email: podixon@podixon.com

Manufactured by Amazon.ca
Bolton, ON